ACKNOWLEDGEMENTS

THANK YOU to all my family and friends who are ALWAYS so supportive during my writing process. It has been a long time coming. A BIG THANK YOU to all my readers. You continue to amaze me with your unwavering support! I am so thrilled to have new content to share with you all and trust me there is more to come. – Xan Tucker (Your favorite author)

DEDICATION

This book is dedicated to anyone who has endured a storm but refused to give up on love. The love that finds after heartbreak is the best. It's always the least expected that lasts a lifetime. Cheers to love and the lifetime of adventure it brings. May we all continue to take up space and show up as our authentic selves. It is in these spaces that true love finds us.

-Xan Tucker

La venganza perfecta

alexis carter

enrique manuel

CHAPTER ONE

It had been one year since I had any communication with Remington Slayton. Well, that was until two weeks ago when I received a fucking wedding invitation from him and his wife. Turns out he actually married Nicole the day he emailed me. Now, they are finally having an official wedding. I'm not sure how my name ended up on the guest list.

The invitation didn't come from Remington himself, per se. It was an evite that came from an email address marked as "The SLAYTONS". While I was over Remington, it still hurt a lot to see that email in my inbox. He was a monster for even sending that bullshit to me. At that moment, I decided to plan a vacation as a gift to myself for surviving a year post-Remington. Man, it took countless therapy sessions, journaling, tears, and overall isolation to get back to my old self. Well, I wasn't really my old self. I was a better version. More aware. Taking up more space. Happier. Horny ass shit, but in a happy place.

Alexis sat patiently at the international terminal at Hartsfield Jackson Airport. After surviving one of the most challenging years of her life, she decided to gift herself a nice vacation. Today was her "survival" anniversary. Everything about the past year had been intentional. Intentional healing. Intentional growing. Intentional alone time. She finally felt like she was getting back to the Alexis Carter that she'd grown to love. The pre-Remington Alexis; but much better than before.

Giddy to spend the next two weeks in Spain. Alexis had so much planned but also incorporated some down time. This was her first solo international trip and while she was nervous, she was also very excited. In addition to this vacation, the previous week Alexis closed on her new house. So, it was a celebration of new beginnings and she was most grateful for them. It wasn't too long ago that Alexis couldn't imagine getting out of the funk she was in…

One year earlier

Remington's email was heart wrenching.

From: Remington Slayton

To: Alexis Carter

Subject: My Last Email

Hey, Alexis. I didn't really expect you to respond to my last email. I know it was a lot to take in and I know how you like to avoid situations you can't control. I also didn't expect for you to block my numbers. I have tried to call and text a few times but I know

you didn't get them. Finally, I didn't expect for you to be moved totally out of the house. You have made it clear where you stand with this relationship.

Thanks for moving out so quickly. It makes it easier for my wife, Nicole, and my son to move in. Yes, we went to the courthouse and got married this morning. I hope you have retrieved all of your items because you are no longer welcome in the Slayton's household. My attorney will be in contact soon.

-R. Slayton

Alexis couldn't believe he had the nerves to send that shit. She wanted to respond to his email so badly but her emotions were so raw and high at the moment that it wouldn't have been good at all. The physical chest pain had returned. This couldn't be life right now. In a state of shock, Alexis stumbled into the therapist's office.

"Hi Alexis, I'm Juanita."

"Nice to meet you, Ms. Juanita."

"Oh, just Juanita is fine. Let's talk about what brings you in today."

Alexis had no idea that one question would be her breaking point. The floodgates opened and she cried for several minutes before responding. Therapists are trained to handle emotional people but she really believed she caught Ms. Juanita off guard with all the crying. She sat patiently and frequently handed Alexis tissues to wipe her eyes and nose. She finally mustered up the energy to give a brief overview of the relationship with Remington and the events that had taken place in the last month.

"I just need help getting my life back together, Ms. Juanita. And I think therapy is a step in the right direction."

One month before she stumbled into her therapist's office, Alexis was at home with her then fiancé celebrating their engagement with family and friends. Things changed so quickly. She barely had time to recognize what was happening. One minute she was enjoying the love Remington had to give and the next minute she was caught up in his destructive path. Alexis didn't recognize her life after the night of the engagement party. She honestly didn't recognize herself.

She spent the last few years loving Remington and his twins. They designed this perfect life for themselves and while it wasn't traditional, it worked. They mapped out what the rest of their lives together would look like and none of that would manifest. Alexis spent years praying for a man like Remington. Praying that God would send her a man who didn't mind protecting, leading, building, and so forth. She also prayed for great sex. God has a sense of humor though. Alexis never thought to pray for an honest, faithful man. The simple things will get you caught up.

Remington was everything Alexis needed and wanted in a man and husband. That was until he wasn't. Until she found out his truth. He wasn't what he pretended to be. They were engaged to be married but he was having an affair with his longtime business partner. Not only were they having an affair but she was pregnant with his child. No one thought to make Alexis privy to this information. It was a fucked-up situation but to make matters worse his "longtime business partner," Nicole, was on Alexis' marketing and public relations team for her books. All thanks to Remington. Alexis wasn't sure what kind of game they were playing but it was sickening.

Nicole couldn't stand the possibility of Remington marrying Alexis, so she decided to air all their dirty laundry the night of the engagement party. This heifer had the nerve to show up at their house (yes, Remington and Alexis bought a house together) during the party. Remington's punk ass had the audacity to leave to diffuse the situation while Alexis had no idea all of this was going on until later that evening. She'd never been so ashamed, humiliated, and embarrassed before in her life. All this happened in front of their families and friends. Getting cheated on is bad enough but to be humiliated in the process is devastating. Alexis wanted to move to Mars in hopes of not having to interact with human beings.

Instead of moving as far away as possible, she took the first step in her healing by going to therapy. Ms. Juanita always tells her how she handled the situation with such grace. There were so many times when she didn't want to be the bigger person. One of the things that helped tremendously was cutting off all contact with Remington. The day he emailed saying he married Nicole was the day Alexis decided she would not give him another second of her life. She blocked his email. Even though they were never friends on social media, she blocked him there as well. The last step was changing her phone number and since Alexis was officially homeless he couldn't just pop up at her house unannounced.

The first three months were pure hell. Alexis didn't sleep, barely ate, and was just functioning in chaos. She spent a lot of time crying, praying for God to take the pain away, and often wondering what Remington was doing. Was he happy with Nicole? How was the baby? But she never caved. Alexis didn't attempt to reach out to him not once and she was damn proud of herself for that. It was difficult breaking the soul-tie with Remington.

CHAPTER TWO

The nine-hour flight to Madrid, Spain finally began the boarding process. Madrid was the first stop on Alexis' two-week vacation. A much needed and well-deserved vacation. Spain had always been on her list of places to visit. She made plans to include it in her honeymoon but didn't get that far. Gathering her things, Alexis headed to the gate. Post-Remington, she made it her business to spoil herself. She had never flown first class on an international flight but decided it was time to change that.

Alexis now understood all the fuss about flying first class. The seats were luxurious and plush with ample leg room. She enjoyed how her body settled into the seat. Alexis grabbed a menu. She was impressed with how extensive it was and she looked forward to ordering her favorite pasta dish and veggies shortly. She couldn't wait to recline her seat later in the flight and enjoy what she hoped to be peaceful sleep. But at this very moment she was looking forward to ordering a cocktail. Again, the offerings in first class were a lot better than general boarding seats. She could get used to traveling like this.

Alexis smiled thinking about how much fun this whole trip was going to be. While she was nervous about traveling alone for such a long period of time, she felt at peace with her decision.

After the flight attendant made the safety announcements, Alexis settled into her seat and pulled out a book. She decided to read *The Year of the Yes by Shonda Rhimes*. When the flight attendant came around to take drink orders, she requested a Jimmy Walker on the rocks. It was difficult to focus on the book because she had so many thoughts running through her mind. She was really doing this. Going to Spain. Alone. This was a sure sign of growth. While Alexis didn't mind doing things alone, traveling out of the country for more than a few days was not one of them.

After her shot and randomly rambling in her journal, Alexis dozed off to sleep. The next time she opened her eyes the pilot was announcing that they were making the final descent into Madrid International Airport. She slept the entire flight. Having missed the meals that were served, Alexis was starving. She knew her first stop after checking into the hotel would be finding food. She would most likely try the restaurant there just to make it quick.

After deplaning the aircraft, she headed to baggage claim. With more than enough packed in her luggage, you would've thought she was moving to Spain permanently. *Which didn't sound like a bad idea.* After baggage claim was passenger pick up. She was greeted by a very nice-looking Spanish man holding a sign that read, "Alexis Carter, welcome to Madrid." She smiled and confirmed that she indeed was Alexis. He grabbed her luggage and headed to the private car that was prearranged for pick up.

"Senorita?"

"Si."

"Tu, hablas español?"

"No."

"Okay, that's fine. You can understand it a little, yes?" She was taken aback by his perfect English-speaking ability. Alexis could tell he knew because he smiled and winked at her.

"Yes, I understand some, but I'm not fluent."

"Not a problem, you'll be fine. Most of us speak English."

"Great, thanks."

Alexis leaned back in the seat and closed her eyes. They were only a short ride from the airport. Her eyes fluttered open as the car slowed. The hotel Alexis had chosen for Madrid was a boutique hotel and screamed charm, history, and just calmness. She knew she made a great choice with this hotel.

The small courtyard faced a historic building that was decorated with greenery growing up the side. There was plenty of seating to enjoy a nice breakfast, lunch, or glass of wine. There were five to six wrought iron tables and chairs out in the courtyard. She particularly enjoyed the color it added to break up the whitewashed brick and stone. The hotel was centrally located but just off the beaten path, so Alexis didn't feel like she was right in the middle of the hustle and bustle that often came with city life. It was quiet and had a calmness about it. She could definitely see herself reading her book and enjoying her hot tea outside at some point during her stay.

She exited the car as the driver grabbed her bags and sat them on the curb. While tipping him, Alexis was happy she converted her US dollars to Euros before leaving Atlanta. That was one less thing to do. Just as she turned to grab her bags from the curb, the bellhop rolled them inside. She walked up to the front desk to check in and was greeted by guest services.

"Welcome to Madrid, Senorita. Carter. Give us a moment to finish your check in."

"Thank you. Of course, take your time."

She wondered how they knew her name. Must be the only black woman staying at this hotel…or the only single person staying at the hotel.

A couple minutes later, Alexis was checked in and heading to her room while her bags were being delivered. The moment she stepped into the room it felt like an oasis created just for her. The calming aroma was welcoming and soothing. She glanced out at the balcony and knew she would spend a few nights enjoying the terrace view. The green space was well maintained and gorgeous. Alexis made her way further into the room and was welcomed by the smell of rose and lavender. The temperature in the room was comfortable and she appreciated that. Alexis hated nothing more than to be too cold or too warm. As she made her way into the bathroom, she was in awe of the spa bath and sitting area. She couldn't wait to relax with a crisp glass of wine after a long day of sightseeing. But that would have to wait until later. Right now, her first order of business was to take a hot, relaxing shower and find something to eat.

CHAPTER THREE

I am confident and brave. I live in the present and look forward to the future.

I deserve to be happy and successful.

Alexis listened to her affirmations while relaxing in the soaker tub. The smell of eucalyptus and rose filled her nostrils. Surrounded by tiny bubbles, she was deep in thought, repeating each affirmation out loud. Indeed, she'd grown.

In a year's time, she let go of her need to control every situation. She now focused on the things that were in her control. She was more self-aware, and this was very helpful as she continued to navigate the temporary feelings that popped up occasionally from her last relationship. Alexis was ready to move forward and be happy in the now, yet she was optimistic about her future. She started doing the hard work in her therapy sessions. Asking the hard, uncomfortable questions and learning more about herself.

After her bath, Alexis decided to get dressed and head downstairs. Starving was an understatement. She made her way to the quaint restaurant and found a window seat. The view of the courtyard was perfect for people watching. There were so many couples, she wondered what their stories were. Remington briefly crossed her mind. She was proud of herself at that moment. She didn't feel sad but relieved that they didn't have a story anymore. Her only desire was a genuine, honest relationship. Definitely not right now though. Alexis enjoyed focusing solely on herself and continuing to heal.

She watched as a black couple cuddled on a swing in the courtyard and she smiled. You would've thought after her last relationship that she had given up on love but the truth is it made her want it even more. The server returned with a chilled glass of wine and pan con tomate. While enjoying her wine and food, she continued to people watch.

Another couple walked through the courtyard holding hands. Alexis let out a deep sigh. She wasn't jealous or envious but definitely didn't have to see this her whole vacation. It wasn't a painful reminder anymore, but she did want a relationship at some point. Feeling her thoughts becoming negative, she quickly quoted her favorite affirmation: *I choose the happiness of this moment over the pain of my past.* A smile touched her lips and all was well. Alexis continued to watch the couples in their own space sharing their happiness with the bystander.

After eating, she decided to venture out and see what was around the hotel. She chose the hotel specifically for its proximity to boutique shops and eateries. After stopping by a pastry shop and grabbing an almond cake, she walked the streets of Madrid and took in the gorgeous architecture of the buildings. People watching had always been her thing. So, people watching in a different culture was fascinating. The body language, the conversations, and the overall interaction was different.

She could tell that the culture in Madrid was a lot slower than in America. No one was rushing to get where they were going. Seemingly, everyone was leisurely strolling. The laughs and talking were a little quieter than what she was accustomed to hearing. Everyone seemed relaxed and less tense and not as stressed. Couples engaged in public affection. She watched as one couple shared light kisses in front of a pastry store after obviously sharing breakfast together.

She found a small table outside a shop and took a break from walking. Not sure how far she'd gone, Alexis made sure not to make any turns. Her sense of direction was horrible. The last thing she needed to do was get lost in the city streets of Madrid. Alexis browsed Viator on her phone to see if there were any additional activities to add to her itinerary. Nothing in particular stuck out but she had a whole week in Madrid and a week in Barcelona. Alexis was sure before her time was up in Madrid that she would find someone who would suggest the hidden gems.

CHAPTER FOUR

After sleeping most of the day before, Alexis could hardly believe it was already day three of her vacation. Finally feeling well-rested, she decided to get up early to go for a three-mile run. Her run provided nice scenery. Madrid was known for its small-town feel. She ran by buildings built in the 1800s that still possessed much of the original character. Each building looked like it had a story to tell. What she particularly enjoyed was running by the small mom and pop shops. She even noticed a fresh fruit and smoothie stand to visit after her run. These stores still had so much character. They weren't modern but you could appreciate the design. Many of them were brick and whitewashed with pops of color. Because she was in the heart of the city, she didn't see much greenery.

After showering, she walked back to the stand for breakfast and enjoyed the views. Alexis walked around a little until she needed her daily nap. She headed back to her hotel where she planned to rest until it was time for her to go back out.

Afterward a much needed nap, she ventured out even more and found a bustling lunch spot about two miles from the hotel. Opting for an outside table, Alexis enjoyed a nice salad and some of the most delicious bread. Luckily, she was walking back to the hotel so she could burn off the calories from all the bread. On her way back to the room, she stopped by the front desk to get a dinner recommendation. The front desk staff unanimously recommended Bodega de los Secretos. Alexis wanted something on the fancier side since she planned to dress up and take herself on a nice dinner date. She always went on one fancy dinner when she was out of the country. This time she planned to do two or more.

The front desk made a reservation for eight o'clock. Alexis headed back to her room and decided to Facetime Brooklyn and Reign. It was time for a check-in and she really wanted to see their faces. They worked her nerves, but she loved them and missed them just a bit.

"Hey y'all!" Alexis smiled into the camera. "I'm checking in."

"Hey Lexie. How is it going?" Brooklyn asked.

"Yeah, what did you do today?" Reign chimed in.

"Not a lot. I did get my run in, had lunch outside, and now I'm relaxing before I head to dinner."

"Oh, sounds fun but not overwhelming," Reign said.

"Is this one of your fancy dinners?" Brooklyn asked.

"Girl yes! I have this bad ass dress. I don't usually do red but this dress is everything!"

"Oh wee, let us see it!" Brooklyn exclaimed.

"Yes, just put it on so we can see this dress," Reign all but screamed.

"Hold tight. Let me put it on real quick."

"Okay," Brooklyn and Reign sung in unison.

Alexis made her way to the bathroom to put on the dress. Quickly slipping the dress on, she took a few extra seconds to admire herself in the mirror. Not to sound arrogant but she looked damn good in that red dress. Alexis propped the phone up on the dresser so Brooklyn and Reign could see the full body. As soon as she stepped back for them to see, Reign did her little signature squeal.

"Damn, that dress is bad as hell," she said.

"Honey, bad is an understatement. You look amazing, Lexie," Brooklyn chimed in.

"Thank y'all. I feel amazing in this dress and can't wait to get all dolled up tonight."

"You'll definitely be turning heads. Don't come back with a Latin man," Brooklyn laughed.

"Nah, come back with a Latin man. That'll be fun," Reign said as she winked.

Reign had no qualms about dating outside her race but Alexis couldn't judge because she definitely had no qualms about dating outside her race either. She smiled at the fond memories that Warner and she shared.

"What has you smiling? Giving some thought to Reign's suggestion?"

"Girl, you know damn well I don't need that suggestion from Reign. I've been there and done that. You might want to take our suggestions, Brooklyn."

"I'm not interested in dating pink toes." Brooklyn rolled her eyes after her statement.

"Well, you're missing out. We know what it's like not to stay on the dark side," Reign said.

"Right. But hey y'all I need to start getting dressed because my black car will be here to pick me up at 7:15."

"Oh, you're just too damn fancy. Black car and shit. Okay then, skank," Reign said.

"Well, take plenty of pics and make sure you check in first thing in the morning," Brooklyn requested.

"I will. Love y'all. Talk to you tomorrow."

"We love you, too," they blurted.

Alexis ended the FaceTime and proceeded to the bathroom. She took the dress off, put it back on the hanger, and slipped into her black silk robe. Luckily, she showered earlier. All she had to do was do a light beat on her face, put her twists in a cute updo, and wear the hell out of this damn dress. Alexis smiled at her reflection in the mirror, so damn proud of herself. She headed to the bathroom to sort through the makeup.

After her makeup was applied and her twists were up, Alexis slipped back into her dress, deciding on her diamond drop earrings, necklace, and bracelet. Her strappy, silver heels and matching clutch added to the accessories. Alexis had on her favorite red lipstick and felt powerful.

Alexis couldn't lie, she was feeling herself. Like a lot. A lot. She stood in the mirror and twirled a few times in her dress. She giggled like a schoolgirl as she did the customary butt look in the mirror. Her workouts were definitely paying off. She admired her toned back and the curves she had gained over the past year.

It had been a while since she felt this damn sexy and welcomed the familiar feeling. She did one final twirl in the mirror before heading out of her hotel room. The looks that she received from staff and other guests confirmed what she felt. The looks from the men let her know she was wearing the hell out of that dress. She walked with confidence and a big smile on her face. One lady looked at her and smiled.

One of the Latin guests spoke in Spanish but the puzzled look on Alexis' face let him know that she didn't understand anything he said. So, he quickly spoke in English. "He shouldn't let you go out alone looking so beautiful, Senorita," he said.

"Thank you, Senor." Then she gave him a wink. He blushed as she sashayed to the front desk.

Sergio, the front desk staff, winked at her with a thumb's up approval. "Senorita. Carter, your car will be here shortly. Do you need anything while you wait?"

"No, Sergio. Thank you."

Alexis waited in the lobby for about five minutes before her car pulled up. She was greeted by her driver as she slid into the backseat. To her surprise, there was a bottle of champagne and an iPod waiting to select her own music. The ride to the restaurant was about thirty-five minutes. So, she decided to do a quick mix of Erykah Badu, Jill Scott, and Ledsi. While sipping champagne, Alexis closed her eyes and got lost in the songs. Before long, they were pulling up to the restaurant.

"Senorita, we are here."

"Gracias."

CHAPTER FIVE

The driver exited the car, opened Alexis' door, and held out his hand. She put her hand in his and stepped out of the car. There wasn't much activity outside the restaurant but she was greeted by a hostess.

"Senorita Carter?"

"Si."

"Bienvenida."

"Gracias."

The ambiance of the restaurant was very intimate and Alexis instantly hoped she hadn't made a mistake by being there. Alone. Alexis listened to the soft music that played just above a whisper. She had no clue what the lyrics were since it was all in Spanish but the melody caused her body to sway naturally. When the server arrived, she ordered water and a glass of wine, continuing her eye tour of the restaurant. The white linen that draped the table accompanied by the softly lit candles definitely set a mood in the place. It screamed of intimacy. Alexis began to feel awkward being the only single person in the restaurant but then she spotted him.

He was tucked away in a corner that was too small for his massive frame. Initially, she only glanced in his direction but instinctively did a double take. Her second glance wasn't a glance at all; it was more like a stare. Hidden in the corner was this fine specimen of a man with an amazing smile, talking on his phone. Alexis wondered who he was talking to and what about. He sipped his drink and she appreciated that he was so engaged in his conversation that he didn't notice her stalker-ish staring. She was brought out of her trance when the server returned to take her order.

Her attention was back on the adonis in the corner as soon as she was done. She felt her breath catch in her throat and her body temperature increase by a degree or two from how attractive he was. Thankfully, she was a darker shade or her cheeks would be red. She was flustered just from looking at him from across the room. *Breathe, Alexis.* The mystery man was at least six feet six inches if she had to guess. The reflection flickered off his honey skin tone. His gorgeous smile was accompanied by a luscious pair of full lips. Alexis appreciated the light shining just enough to highlight his features. When she thought his appearance couldn't get any better, she finally noticed the massive curls atop his head. He had the sides and back tapered cut. She appreciated his round, alert eyes and thick, almost perfect eyebrows. He was just a fine man. Breaking her gaze, Alexis took a sip of water. Clearly, she was thirsty by the way she was staring at this man. She even strained in an attempt to hear his conversation but he clearly did not want to be heard.

Alexis waited patiently for the server to return with her food. Honestly, she didn't have an appetite for food anymore. All she could think about was the mystery man sitting in this quaint restaurant alone. At least they had that in common. Her food arrived and she all but picked at it before having the waitress box it up. She sat a few moments in deep thought about life. Alexis couldn't lie like she was always excited about the future because she was not. So much happened in a year's time. Some days she navigated those emotions well but other days she struggled. Right now, she felt guilty for not being excited. Hell, she was on one of her dream vacations and had just purchased her dream home. Alexis felt selfish and ungrateful. *Okay Alexis, get it together. No more pity parties on vacation.*

Finishing her glass of wine, she got up from the table while digging into her purse for her phone. She would ask a waitress to take her picture in this sexy ass dress in front of the restaurant. Or she could get someone outside to take it. She opted for the latter.

Making her way outside, Alexis asked the nice gentleman at the valet booth to take her picture. Just as they finished she heard a thunderous voice say, *"Ms. Carter?"*

Alexis turned and came face to face with the monstrosity of a man also known as the mystery man from the corner of the restaurant.

"Yes, I'm Alexis Carter."

"Great, you left without getting your credit card back."

"Oh, thank you."

"You're welcome."

He handed her card back and it wasn't until then that it dawned on her that he spoke perfect English. "Wait, are you American?" Alexis noticed the puzzled look on his face. She actually liked how his eyebrows grew in closer as he gave a sly smile as if he didn't expect that question from her.

"I'm Spanish American. Is that an issue?" He asked with a smirk.

"No, I just assumed you were Spanish. I wasn't expecting you to speak fluent English."

"Well, I am Spanish. And you Americans realize nearly everyone speaks fluent English, right?"

"You, Americans?"

He threw his hands up. "I'm only kidding. My dad is Spanish and my mom is African American."

"Oh, okay. Well, thanks for returning my card. My car should be here soon. I don't want to waste anymore of your time."

"Not a waste of time actually. I'm happy to see such a beautiful face tonight."

Oh, he was flirting. This was not a game he wanted to play.

"I'm sure you see plenty of beautiful faces."

Alexis was a flirt by nature and she could tell he was flirting with her. She stood a little taller and did a quick lick of her lips. What she really wanted to do was make sure her lipstick was still in place. While she enjoyed flirting, she couldn't pretend like this unnamed god didn't make her a tad bit nervous. She nibbled on the inside of her jaw and let her eyes look everywhere but on him. Until they did. And she enjoyed every sight of him.

"Not like yours though. I've seen some beautiful Spanish women but not many beautiful black women."

"Umm, okay."

"Do you have plans after this? I would love to continue our conversation."

"I don't have plans but I've already called for my car."

"You can cancel it and call for another later?"

"Can I? I don't even know your name."

"Oh right, sorry. I'm Enrique Manuel."

She heard a bit of southern drawl in his voice and it caught her off guard. "Do you live here in Madrid or are you visiting?"

"I'm visiting. I visit a few times a year. I was raised in Texas. I live in Austin. What about you?"

"I was born and raised in Tennessee but I live in Atlanta."

There was something oddly familiar about him. Alexis visited Austin last year but she was certain she would have remembered him. There's no woman in her right mind that would have forgotten this man. Had they met somewhere else? Or did she just want a connection to him? It was all odd.

"Hello, do you want me to cancel your car?"

"Umm, sure why not? Will we continue the conversation inside the restaurant? It's a little chilly out here."

"Yes, I'll get us to a private room."

Enrique walked away as Alexis gathered her thoughts. Despite it being a little chilly, she could feel the sweat gathering under her nose as she played with one of her twists that was pulled loose. She only did these things under two circumstances: when she was about to speak publicly or when she got nervous around someone's fine ass son.

CHAPTER SIX

Enrique stood in the entrance of the restaurant while Alexis stood in the same spot he left her in. He took a few seconds to admire her from behind. The moment she entered the restaurant Enrique was alerted to her presence. His body responded immediately. He also noticed her staring at him which he didn't mind one bit. If his mom hadn't been talking his ear off, he would have made his way to her table. He licked his lips and shook his head as he made the few steps it took to get back to her.

She had no idea how sexy she was in that dress that he was sure was tailored just for her. There's no way it wasn't custom made. It hugged every curve. If it hadn't been red, it would have easily been mistaken as a part of her being. It fit just that well. He hadn't been lying when he said he didn't see beautiful black women often while visiting his second home.

Enrique approached Alexis and placed her hand in his. He noticed how she tensed at his touch. Hopefully, it was the surprise of him touching her and not repulsive. The latter would be hard for him to fathom since she had been eyeing him the entire time she was eating her dinner.

"Hey, are you ready to head back inside?" Enrique asked.

"Yes, were you able to get a private room?" Alexis countered his question.

"It wasn't a matter of if, but when," he said with a smirk.

"What are you VIP here or something?" Alexis asked.

"Something like that. Not too important but important enough."

Enrique didn't feel a need to let her know the restaurant was owned by his family. While a few of their cousins invested in the restaurant, his dad, Jorge, and uncle, Jose, were the majority owners.

He kept her hand in his as he led her down the stairs to the private suites that were usually booked. Enrique had gotten lucky that one was readily available. The staircase was wide enough for him and Alexis to walk side by side so he made the extra step or two to be by her side but he never let her hand go. Oddly, he found comfort in touching her in such an intimate way. She seemed to be a bit more relaxed and not as tense underneath his hand.

He noticed she wasn't saying much but she was admiring the artwork and the ambiance of the stairwell. Most of the artwork was from renowned Spanish artists. Never had Enrique appreciated the dim lit stairwell as much as he did at this moment. He looked at Alexis as she studied the artwork. The dim lights allowed him to see the small freckles that sprinkled her face. She also had a few moles that he wanted to reach out and touch, in particular the mole on her neck.

They finally reached the landing and Enrique headed to Suite 333. He always considered three to be his lucky number and now he knew it was. Entering the code to the keyless entry, reluctantly he let Alexis hand go, stepped aside once the door was opened, and allowed Alexis to step into the room first. The table was draped in a white tablecloth and adorned with candles. The chairs were covered with white chair covered with gold accessories. Most of the pictures in the room were abstract art in metallic covers with gold frames. The room also had a white leather sofa with gold accent pillows. This particular room had a view of the underground terrace that was only open a few months out of the year. The view was amazing. He knew Alexis was awed by it because of the smile she wore.

Enrique did like the fact that whether the terrace was in use or not the view was always amazing. The string lights lined the enclosed gazebo and the white linen was changed frequently throughout the day. During the evening hours, the tables were also adorned with candles. It was a vibe outside.

He watched as Alexis walked over to the window and her eyes lit up as she gazed out in awe of this hidden gem. She slowly turned from the window and took in the room. Enrique enjoyed watching her body move so smoothly as she did a little spin to take it all in. In the center of the sofa table sat a beautiful bouquet of flowers. Alexis was immediately drawn to the sunflower in the middle. Sunflowers were her favorite flower.

Enrique continued to watch in awe as she moved gently throughout the small room. He appreciated the way she took in every inch of the space. Most people would stand in the door and assume they had a full view but they would miss the small details. He could stand there and watch her all night but that would be a gross waste of his time. And he didn't want to waste any time when it came to this brown goddess. As Alexis continued to get acquainted with the small space, Enrique walked over to the iPad and Bluetooth speaker in the corner to turn on some music.

"Do you have a preference on music?"

"Not really. Let me see what your taste in music is like."

"Okay, but I asked you first."

Alexis looked up at him and smiled as she made her way to the leather sofa. She laid her silver clutch on the table. She held her phone in her hand. At that moment, Enrique would have paid to feel her fingers on him. He noticed her looking at her phone.

"Do you need to check in with someone?"

"No, I was thinking about texting my best friends a picture of this private room but I know they will want more details."

Enrique chuckled. "That's probably best for after this. I would like your undivided attention."

Alexis was startled when she heard Al Green coming from the speakers. When she looked up, Enrique had a smirk on his face. He had known his music choice would shock her.

He made his way to the sofa and sat on the opposite side, stretching his long legs out in front of him. He peeped Alexis admiring his muscular thighs. He was happy with his wardrobe choice. He had on fitted black slacks and a black button down that complimented his biceps. He had been referred to as fine a time or two but the way

Alexis kept stealing glances he would be inclined to believe that she enjoyed looking at him.

"How tall are you, Enrique?"

"I'm 6'5. Both my dad and uncle are 6'6. We are the three tallest out of the family."

"Oh, wow. You know I have to ask the cliché question." Enrique looked at Alexis with a raised eyebrow but didn't say anything. He knew what she was about to ask. "Did you play basketball?"

"No, but I did high jump and I was on the swim team. What about you? Did you play any sports growing up? What do you do to keep in shape because you are definitely in shape."

He noticed Alexis shifted in her seat a little at the mention of her physique. Did that make her uncomfortable? Surely, she had heard that before and much more.

"Nope, no sports for me. I took up running and biking later in life so those are my go-to for staying in shape. And of course, eating halfway decent."

Damn, she was a runner. Was God trying to tell him something or give him a sign about Alexis? He didn't meet too many women, especially black women that ran for fun consistently.

"Nice. What's your preferred distance?"

Enrique could tell his question sparked interest in Alexis. She sat up a little taller and smiled at him.

"I prefer half marathons but I run three to five miles regularly. I tried marathons and I'll say not so much."

"I can understand that. My preferred distance is 10K. By the 5K mark, I'm just warming up but by the 10K mark I'm ready to call it quits. It's my sweet spot."

"How often do you run?"

"A few times per week but I also love lifting heavy in the gym. I don't want too much cardio to counteract the work I put in at the gym."

"Oh, okay. Any parks you recommend for running while here?"

"I have a few favorite running routes. How long are you here for? Maybe we can run together before you head back home."

"I have four more days here then I'm going to Barcelona for a week before heading back to Atlanta."

"Nice. You'll like Barcelona if you like New York. If you don't have plans in the morning, let's meet for a three mile run."

"Sounds good. Now, let me get to know more about you before I go on this random run with this random guy."

They laughed. Enrique didn't want to show how excited he was that he would get to spend a little more time with Alexis. Hell, if it was up to him, he would become her personal tour guide for the next four days. Maybe he should put a plan in place to do just that. Who better to show her his city than him?

CHAPTER SEVEN

Enrique and Alexis fell into an organic conversation. She was definitely comfortable around him. His vibe was good. Shit, he was fine, too, but it was more than his looks. His conversation was great and they didn't have the awkward moments of silence most strangers would have. She was nervous initially, especially when he rested his hand on the small of her back as they were heading to the private room. Not nervous at his touch but nervous because her body responded instantly. It had been a long while since she had that kind of response to a man's touch. Hell, who was she kidding? It had been a while since she had felt a man's touch.

"How did you end up in Atlanta?" he asked.

"After I finished undergrad at FAMU, I decided to attend Georgia State University for graduate school."

"Oh, so you're a fellow HBCU alumni?" Enrique plastered a smile on his face. It was sexy as hell and he probably had no idea.

"Which school did you attend?"

"I attended Prairie View A&M but I did my graduate school studies at the University of Texas."

"What did you study?"

"I studied architecture at Prairie View and I obtained my master's in Engineering from UT. What about you? What did you study?"

"In undergrad, I obtained my bachelor's in Political Science and African American studies, with a minor in legal studies. I know I was all over the place but I had genuine interest in all three. Plus, my goal was to attend law school. I did the dual program at Georgia State for my Master's in Public Administration and my JD. But I decided practicing law wasn't for me."

"So, what do you do for work?"

Alexis appreciated the attentive look Enrique gave her. His round eyes were a turn on. His pupils were so dark. His eyes added to his sexiness. She could get lost in the moment just staring into his eyes.

"I work as a consultant for government organizations and non-profit organizations. I help them with structural reorganization to maximize resources and profits."

"What company do you work for?"

"Well, I work for Carter Enterprises, LLC now. Last year, I decided to do my own thing and expanded my services to non-profit organizations. It's been challenging but worth it."

"Oh, I see. I'm sure that was a smart move."

"What about you? I'm sure you are utilizing your engineering degree."

Enrique smiled and she could see him light up as she took in every inch of his body. He was a massive man. She loved how on several occasions she caught a glimpse of his quads flexing underneath his dress pants.

"I work for EM & Co. It's a small engineering firm. So, I do a little bit of everything. I love it because it allows me to be hands on."

"You mean EM & Co as in Enrique Manuel & Company?" Enrique wore a smirk on his face and nodded slowly. "Why didn't you just say you were the CEO & Owner?"

"Does it matter?"

"No, but it seems like you were being secretive about it. What other secrets do you have, Senor Manuel?"

He smiled at her and said, "I have no secrets but I'm not an open book either. Feel free to ask me what you want to know." Alexis rolled her eyes at him before picking up her phone and checking the time. It was a little after eleven. She would definitely call for her car by midnight.

"You have somewhere to be?"

"No, I just don't want it to get too late and I can't get car service."

"Oh, that won't be a problem. We have car services that run as long as the restaurant is open and we don't close until one o'clock."

"We?"

"Yes, this is a family-run establishment."

"As in your family? Yet, another secret."

"Yes, my family, but it's not a secret. My dad and uncle are the owners."

Alexis' thoughts were interrupted when Johnnie Taylor's, Good Love, came through the speakers. Instinctively, she started singing the words. She could tell he was amused at how she was so engrossed in the song. He rested his hand on her thigh palm up.

"Dance with me?" he asked with anticipation.

"I really don't dance," Alexis responded.

"Come on. You're on vacation. Have some fun," he said, smiling.

"Umm, okay. I guess."

Enrique stood and then pulled Alexis to her feet. Until that moment, she hadn't noticed a small remote on the table. He quickly hit the back button and started the song over.

CHAPTER EIGHT

The moment Alexis' body made contact with his, Enrique knew she was a force to be reckoned with. Hell, who was he kidding? He knew that the moment she walked into the restaurant. Alexis stepped into his personal space and he wished he could get her even closer. Her feminine scent complimented by the perfume she wore filled his nostrils. His body responded by rising a couple degrees in temperature. They fell into a good rhythm and he felt her relax after a couple minutes. One dance was not enough for him. When the song ended he asked her to continue. Surprisingly, she agreed.

Enrique decided to change the music to 90's R&B. Something he figured they both would enjoy. The first song to come through the speakers was Usher, Nice and Slow. Alexis gave him a smile and stepped back into his personal space. It could have been his imagination but it seemed she was a little closer this time. She rested her head in the middle of his chest, even with heels on he still towered over her. Her dress was low cut so when he placed his hand on the small of her back, his fingertips made contact with her bare skin. Enrique felt

Alexis shiver at the contact but she didn't tense up.

Alexis was sure Enrique would feel her heart pounding from the contact of his fingers on her bare skin. His touch was warm. She leaned closer to his body and relished in the feel of his muscular frame pressing every so lightly against hers. The only two thoughts in her mind were: she could do this for hours and she enjoyed melding her body into his. They danced through another three or four songs before Enrique finally pulled away.

"We need to get you back to your hotel before I have you here all night," Enrique said.

Alexis could tell he was conflicted by the look in his eyes. Honestly, she would have been okay with being there with him all night, melded into his body, enjoying his touch.

"Right, that would be a smart idea," she finally responded.

"I'll have the staff upstairs to call your car. It'll be a few minutes before they arrive so we don't have to head back up just yet," he informed her.

"Okay." That was all Alexis could muster up. She walked back to the white leather sofa and sat down. She looked at her phone out of habit. It was at that moment she realized that she didn't get enough pictures in her dress. Once Enrique finished speaking with the staff upstairs, Alexis would ask him to take her picture.

"Hey, can you do me a favor and take a few pics of me in my dress?" Alexis asked.

It could have been her imagination but his eyes seemed to darken even more. She was certain that Enrique found her attractive. She noticed how he would quickly glance in her direction from time to time. She also noticed that he wanted their bodies just as close as she did when they were dancing. It was safe to say the attraction was mutual.

"Of course. You want to start by the window? We can even take a couple out on the terrace, too," Enrique said.

"That would be great," she responded.

Ten minutes later, Alexis had enough pics in this red dress to last her a lifetime. She had the memory of dancing with Enrique to last her a lifetime, too. She had to admit that he gave great instructions on posing and position for the right lighting for the pictures. He had done well. She couldn't wait to share them with her crew in the morning.

"Do you still plan to go running with me in the morning?" Enrique asked.

"What time?"

"What time works best for you? My schedule is wide open."

"Let's do 10 then."

"That works. I'll need your number to call you to arrange a pick-up." Enrique winked at her. Alexis rattled off her number and he saved it in his cell phone. Then her phone started ringing.

"Lock my number in please."

"Sure."

"Your car should be here soon. Let's head upstairs."

Alexis headed towards the door and up the stairs. Enrique didn't walk side by side with her the way they had done on their way down. He instead trailed behind her. Alexis was concentrating so hard and praying that she didn't have a mishap that would cause her to fall backwards. She exhaled a breath that she didn't realize she was holding when she reached the landing. Enrique placed his hand at the small of her back and walked her to the valet booth.

It was his touch. It felt amazing and she was sure she would dream about it tonight. It warmed her body and reminded her that she was alive with needs that had been unmet for too long. Any other time, the warning alarms would be going off in her head but she didn't feel the need to warn herself of the last time she had such a strong connection to someone.

"It was my pleasure spending the evening with you, Senorita. Looking forward to our run later this morning."

"Likewise, Senor Emanuel. I'll be up by nine o'clock so feel free to shoot me a text with the details for the run."

"I will." He leaned in and placed a kiss on her cheek and then her forehead. As he pulled back, her black car pulled up. Enrique walked over and opened her door, stepping aside to allow her to slide in. Afterwards, he winked and closed the door.

Alexis noticed the driver smiling at her.

"Senorita, it's about a half hour drive back to your hotel. There's an iPad for you to select your music. Relax and I'll have you at your destination shortly."

"Thank you."

Alexis laid her head back and closed her eyes. She didn't need any music. She actually didn't want to interrupt her thoughts while she replayed the night she'd just spent with the Spanish American that is known as Enrique Manuel. She loved that he was gentle, yet masculine. Serious, yet playful.

And it didn't hurt that he was very easy on the eyes and smelled divine. It would be a long night.

CHAPTER nine

Enrique took a shower once he made it back to his apartment. The smell of Alexis still caressed his nostrils and his fingertips could still feel the warmth from her chocolate brown skin. Skin that he imagined his lips massaging. He shook his head to rid himself of his thoughts. It would be a long night if he didn't get his mind right. He decided to text Alexis for the address to her hotel and to let her know a car would pick her up at 9:15 in the morning.

Enrique: Hey did you make it back to your hotel okay? Also, send me the address to your hotel.

Alexis: Hi. I was just thinking about you. Yes, I made it back.

Alexis pinged her location so he would have the address.

Enrique: Oh, so you were thinking about me? Hope it was good thoughts.

Alexis: Of course. You haven't given me a reason to have bad thoughts.

Enrique: Good because I was thinking about you as well. Can I ask you something?

Alexis: Shoot for it.

Enrique: Well, a couple questions that may lead to other questions.

Alexis: Oh boy. Go ahead.

Enrique: What's the perfume you were wearing tonight? It smelled divine on you.

Alexis blushed at his question. Of course, she wore her favorite perfume. It was good to know that he appreciated it as much as she does.

Alexis: Jimmy Choo. Next question.

Enrique: Is it safe for me to assume you aren't seriously involved with anyone back home?

Alexis: Absolutely safe to assume that but you might not want to get in the habit of making assumptions.

Enrique: Sarcasm?

Alexis: Just a tad bit. So, is it safe for me to assume you aren't seriously involved with anyone back home or here in Spain?

Enrique: Yes, just don't get in the habit of making assumptions. ☺

Alexis: I saw that coming. How long do you plan to stay in Spain?

Enrique: I'm thinking another three weeks. I'll head back right before the firm starts work on a new contract we were recently awarded.

Alexis: Oh cool. I have four more days including tomorrow and then I'm headed to Barcelona for a week.

Enrique: You need to let me show you around since you haven't been to many of the local spots to experience the real culture.

Alexis: I would love that only if you have time. I know you are busy with family and helping out at the restaurant.

Enrique: I'm on vacation just like you. I just happen to vacation in the city where my family lives.

Alexis: Great. We can discuss it on our run in a few hours. Speaking of what time should I be ready?

Enrique: 9:15. I'll have a car pick you up. Get some rest and I'll see you later.

Alexis: Same to you. Good night.

She couldn't hide the smile on her face. She would be spending the next few days with Enrique. Excited didn't begin to describe how she felt. She was giddy like a schoolgirl as her mind began racing. What would he look like in his running clothes? Where would he take her? Did he do this for other girls? Shit, she didn't want to think about that. She just wanted to live in the moment and it was a marvelous moment. Her thoughts picked back up. Would he hold her hand again? *Oh God, I hope he holds my hand again.* She was almost too excited to fall asleep thinking about spending the upcoming days with him.

She had already showered and was lounging in her silk red robe. Alexis poured a glass of wine to calm her nerves and here she was excited all over again. It was well after 1 AM and she was wide awake. This hadn't been the case since she made it to Spain. She didn't have any issue with getting her rest.

It was a little after seven in Atlanta and a little after six for her mom in Tennessee. She decided to text Brooklyn and Reign pictures of her in the red dress.

Alexis: Did I wear the hell out of this dress or what?

Reign: Sis, you look amazing. How was dinner?

Brooklyn: You know you wore that damn dress. The better question is who took these shots of you?

Alexis blushed at the thought of the mini photo shoot she and Enrique had before she left the restaurant.

Reign: Great question, Brooklyn. So, who took the picture?

Alexis: Enrique. I met him at the restaurant and we decided to hang out a little to talk.

Brooklyn: First of all, don't be texting this to us. This is worthy of a FaceTime call.

Alexis: I'm heading to bed. It is after 1 AM and I'm getting up to run in the morning with Enrique.

Reign: See this is what I like to hear!

Brooklyn: We need details as soon as it's an appropriate time for us in the morning.

Reign: Yes, we do. I need to see a picture of him.

Alexis: I don't have a picture of him.

Brooklyn: Take one tomorrow after your run. Ain't that what y'all runners like to do. Document you actually ran?

Alexis: Shut up, Brooklyn. I'll see what I can do though.

Reign: Make sure we get the picture first so the story will make sense in our heads.

Alexis: You are so damn silly girl but I will. I love y'all.

Brooklyn: Love you too, Lexie.

Reign: Love you too, Senorita Carter. ☺

Alexis: You sound like Enrique. Good night.

Alexis decided to send her mom a few quick text messages and a couple pictures from tonight. She didn't hear a response immediately but knew by morning she would have heard back from her.

CHAPTER TEN

Alexis was dragging the next morning. It was way too early for her to be up and she was in no mood to be running at the moment. She quickly dressed and headed downstairs to wait for Enrique's car to arrive. She was tired yet giddy as hell to see him again. Her mind already wondered what he would look like sweaty. She couldn't wait to see him in action.

Alexis glanced at her phone wondering why her mom hadn't responded to her text messages last night. That was definitely not like her. She made a mental note to FaceTime her and to also FaceTime her sister, Monica. Alexis was in the lobby maybe five minutes before a black car pulled up for her. *Does everyone use black cars around here?* She walked out of the lobby to where the driver was holding the door open for her.

"Buenos días, Señorita Carter."

"Si, buenos días. Hablas ingles?"

"Yes, senorita. We are heading to El Retiro Park."

"Okay, thank you."

"Senor Manuel will already be at the park."

Alexis nodded and began scrolling on social media. She hadn't been this excited about running in a while, despite the chill in the air. The park was only a twenty-minute drive from her hotel. The black car pulled into the first entrance and there he stood. Enrique had on running shorts and a short sleeve shirt. So much for her seeing his long six-foot six-inch frame in running tights. She had actually been anticipating that moment. The car rolled to a stop and Enrique walked over and opened her door.

"Good Morning, Ms. Carter," he said.

"Good Morning, Senor Emanuel."

He thanked the driver and said something in Spanish. The driver nodded and drove off. Enrique turned to Alexis with a big smile.

"Are you ready to do this?" he asked.

"Yes, but what park is this again? The driver told me but I can't remember," she said.

"El Retiro Park. It's a great area for running short and mid distances and has great scenery. You'll enjoy it," he responded.

"Okay but wait! What's your mile time because I'm not fast. I mean, I'm not slow either," she said.

"I'm about a 7:45 – 8:15 average mile time on a good day," Enrique said.

"I'm about a 9:00 – 9:30 average mile time on a good day," Alexis responded.

"We will consider this your tempo run for the week then," he said while laughing.

"Oh really?" Alexis frowned.

They both took a moment to do quick stretches and set their watches. Alexis knew she would not be keeping up with Enrique, especially not at his pace. She already decided that as long as she kept him in sight, she would be okay. She also knew the view from behind would be an enjoyable one so she couldn't even be mad.

"Ready?" Enrique asked. They had already decided to run three miles the day before.

Alexis nodded her head and they took off. As she figured, Enrique's takeoff was faster than her normal pace. Surprisingly, she kept up with him for the first mile. She looked at her watch and her mile time was 8:17. However, she knew she needed to slow down if she intended to make it the entire three miles. She slowed her pace to 8:40 and Enrique slowed his pace as well. The pace was still too fast for her to hold a conversation. It truly was a tempo run. Along the way, Enrique pointed out certain things and provided a bit of history for her. She appreciated him doing so and was happy he didn't expect her to say anything back. Her watch chimed indicating she had hit the two-mile mark and her average pace was 8:24. She was still moving too fast but she didn't feel bad. She actually felt pretty good.

Around mile two and a half, they spotted a group training. You could tell they were elites. Enrique knew a couple of the guys in the group. So, he picked up his pace. Alexis maintained her impromptu tempo run pace. When her watch chimed indicating mile three, she looked at the average pace and was shocked to see 8:20. It was then that she realized she was tired. She stopped and spotted Enrique talking with two guys from the training group. She took a minute to catch her breath and to stretch as she was sure she would feel the effects from the run in a day or two.

Enrique made his way to her. She noticed his curls were now damp and almost matted to his head. She enjoyed seeing the sweat run down this face and could only imagine how the sweat traveled to his muscular chest.

"How do you feel?" he asked.

"I'm a little tired but not as bad as I thought I would," she responded.

"Great, what's your plan for the rest of the day?"

"No plans but to take a hot shower," Alexis said.

It could have been her imagination but she thought she saw his pupils darken at the mention of taking a shower. Maybe her mind was playing tricks on her. Or so she thought until he licked his lips. Lord, what she would pay to have her tongue licking his full, gorgeous lips. While she had imagined what he would look like sweaty, surprisingly he wasn't as sweaty after the run. He didn't seem the least bit tired or winded during the run. If she didn't know any better, she would think he was running conservatively at that pace.

"Okay, do you need to head back to your hotel to shower or are you up for a little adventure?" Enrique asked. The look on his face told Alexis whatever he had planned would definitely be adventurous.

Alexis, never the one to turn down any fun or adventure, decided on the latter. "I'm always up for a little adventure."

"Great, we're headed to the other side of the park," Enrique said.

Alexis didn't say anything. She just followed his lead. She realized she had a hard time keeping up with his walking pace due to his long legs. It felt like a slight jog to her. After walking for about eight minutes, she spotted the adventure before he said anything. They were going to rent bikes. She enjoyed riding her bike in a controlled environment like a trail or bike park. She looked at Enrique and saw the smirk on his face. The mischievous look on his face told her the environment would most likely not be controlled. They would not be bike riding on the trail they had just run.

"Where are we riding these bikes?" she asked.

"Just around this area," Enrique responded.

"Outside of the park?" she quizzed him.

"Yes. Is that a problem?" he asked.

"Yes and no. I just get nervous when I'm not in a controlled environment," Alexis responded.

"No, worries. Bike riders are just as respected as runners," he replied.

Alexis didn't say anything but she could feel her anxiety rising. The palms of her hands were sweaty which was a clear indication that her anxiety level had risen. She licked her lips and suddenly realized how thirsty she was.

"Is there somewhere we can get a bottle of water?" she asked.

"Can you hold off for about ten minutes? The place we are headed to will have water," Enrique responded.

"Yes, that's fine."

At least she now knew they weren't going a long distance on the bike. That gave her some kind of relief. Not a lot because she didn't know if they would be riding with a lot of car traffic. Why hadn't she paid attention to see if the streets had designated bike lanes before now? One thing she noticed was the traffic wasn't as fast paced as Atlanta. Hopefully, that meant she would make it to their destination safely. Alexis was so into her thoughts she hadn't realized Enrique was talking.

"I'm sorry, what did you say?" Alexis asked.

"Are you up for the bike ride?"

"Yes, let's do this."

The smile that touched Enrique's lips was worth the risk she was about to take. He paid for the bikes and provided her with quick directions just so she would know. Not that it mattered to her because her sense of direction was horrible. She would get lost making all right turns. Somehow, she would make a left turn somewhere. It would be imperative that she keep up with him. They grabbed their bikes and hopped on. Alexis giggled at seeing Enrique's massive frame on the bike. He had chosen the biggest bike they had but it still seemed a little small for him. She began following him. They exited the park and made a right. Surprisingly, this took them through a residential neighborhood.

Enrique pointed out architectural designs and gave little history lessons here and there. They rode in the neighborhood making random turns for about a mile. When they exited the neighborhood, they were back on a busier street. Thankfully, it had designated bike lanes and there were quite a few others out riding their bikes. The further they rode the less traffic and the streets became much narrower. Soon they were in an area with lots of shops, restaurants, and more pedestrians.

They finally stopped in front of a smoothie shop. The smile on Alexis' face let Enrique know how excited she was. Hopping off the bike, Alexis began to chain it to the station. She saw Enrique smirking but didn't care. She was thirsty and wanted something of sustenance. He chained his bike and they headed into the shop. Alexis perused the menu as she stood at the front counter while Enrique was engaged in a friendly conversation. He obviously was a regular here. She placed her order for a peach mango smoothie, bottled water, and smoked salmon on toast. Enrique ordered a smoothie, an omelet, and bottled water. They grabbed a table near the back with a view of the street. He pulled her chair out and their hands brushed lightly against each other. Alexis' body instantly warmed a degree or two. She could tell he felt the electric sensation as well.

CHAPTER ELEVEN

"What are your plans for Barcelona?" Enrique asked.

"I haven't decided yet. I just know I'm exploring the city and seeing what I can get into," Alexis replied.

"I can give you a few recommendations but I suggest coming back when the weather is nicer so you can check out their beaches," he said.

"Sounds interesting. What do you suggest I do while there?"

Enrique provided her with quite a bit to do. His recommendations sounded reasonable and she would still have time to relax. She definitely needed to find a fancy restaurant so she could dress up again. She smiled at the thought of wearing her gold dress.

"What has you smiling over there?" Enrique asked.

"I'm thinking about what I'm going to wear when I take myself on another fancy dinner," Alexis responded. She was blushing and Enrique loved it.

"Oh, so you do this all the time then? Dress up and go to fancy restaurants?"

"Yes, I usually travel with my sister, Monica, or my two best friends, Reign and Brooklyn. This is my first solo trip."

"Why the switch up?"

Alexis stared into space for a moment before answering him. "Last year was challenging and I just needed a getaway as a celebration for surviving the year but also because I just purchased my dream home."

"Oh, nice. If you don't mind me asking what made it so challenging?"

"An ugly breakup with enough drama to last me a lifetime."

"Oh, okay. I get it."

They both sat quietly for a moment. It was a comfortable silence, not an awkward one. Alexis stared out the window in deep thought of the events over the past year. She was definitely proud of how far she had come. Not wanting it to get awkward, she decided to ask him some questions.

"Do you ever think you will leave Austin?"

"I doubt it. As long as my mom is there, I'll most likely be there. Like me, she's an only child."

"Oh, okay. So, you are a momma's boy?"

"Not at all, but I have an amazing relationship with my mom and I'm not sure I want her living in a city all alone with no family. We have no immediate family in Austin. We have a few cousins in Dallas and Houston though."

"That's understandable. My mom still has family in Mississippi and my brother and his wife live within an hour drive. My sister lives in Memphis, which is the closest major city to my small hometown."

"And you are the baby, correct?"

"Yes, I am. Mom and Dad closed shop after me." Alexis giggled.

"Were your parents ever married?"

"Yes, they were but they divorced when I was a teenager. Mom never remarried but Dad did. What about your parents?"

"No, they never married. Mom and I would come to Spain every summer until I was teenager and she felt comfortable letting me travel alone. But she always visits Spain at least two weeks out of the summer."

"She loves it that much, huh?"

"Yes and no. She was an intern when she met my dad here. So, she made some lifelong friends. They still get together in the summer when she's out of school."

"Oh, that's great. After all these years they keep in touch. What does your mom teach?"

"She's a professor at the University of Texas in their architecture department. She loves it."

"Oh, that's nice. And what about your dad?"

"Dad is really a mogul. You know he's part owner of the restaurant. He also has real estate investments throughout Madrid and Barcelona but his passion is architecture, too."

"Nice. So, you followed in the footsteps of your parents, huh?"

"Not really. Don't get me wrong I love architecture but I love the engineering side of things, too. It's a nice balance."

Alexis went quiet while thinking about her passion for writing and how she missed being the creative that she is. "It has been difficult for me to get back to being creative. I just haven't felt it. I'm hoping this getaway can re-energize that part of me."

"Hmm, creative. What are you creating? Maybe I can help you with that," Enrique said as he winked.

"I'm a writer. I like to write poetry, romance, urban fiction, etc. Do you still think you can help, Senor Manuel?"

Alexis didn't mind flirting at all. Honestly, she wouldn't mind taking it a bit further but she didn't want to get beside herself. Not yet anyway.

"I'm sure after I show you all the fun places and expose you to some things tourists usually don't experience you'll have plenty of writing material."

Alexis was a little disappointed with his response. She was hoping for something a little more enticing and flirtatious. She giggled at herself. Here she was being all thirsty.

"Are you up for dinner tonight? I'm thinking we can go to the oldest restaurant in the world, Sobrino de Botin," Enrique asked.

"Oh yes, that was on my list to visit. I'd love to go tonight."

"Great, I'll get you back to your hotel so you can rest and I'll have a car pick you up tonight at 7."

"Sounds like a great plan."

Alexis wore the biggest grin on her face. Her disappointment from just a few moments earlier was now a thing of the past. Enrique smiled at the simple fact that she was smiling. They finished their food and got back on their bikes to head back to the park. He knew the car would be there soon to pick them up.

CHAPTER TWELVE

Alexis was well rested after her nap. She was getting dressed when her mom finally decided to return her phone call.

"Hi, Mom."

"Hey baby. How is Spain?" Alexis could tell her mom sounded tired. She didn't sound like her normal chippy self.

"Spain is fine. Are you okay? You sound exhausted."

"Yes, I've been really tired lately. I have a doctor's appointment next week."

"Are you going to the doctor because you're tired or is something else going on?"

"Just tired but no matter how much rest I get I'm still tired. Hoping my iron isn't low."

"Mom, have you been taking your vitamins?"

"Yes, Alexis. I've been taking my vitamins, getting plenty of sleep, drinking water, eating properly, and I'm still tired."

Alexis didn't press the issue because she could hear the frustration in her mom's voice. She didn't want to make a fuss out of nothing. "Okay. I'm glad you have made an appointment then."

"Yes, I figured everyone would want me to make one so I'm a step ahead of y'all today."

Alexis laughed at her mom's comment. She knew her three children would be on her behind about getting to the doctor. Alexis didn't say anything to her mom but she was concerned. She sounded very tired.

"Thanks for returning my phone call. You sound really tired so I'll let you get some rest. I'll text you later to check on you."

"I'm okay, baby girl. Give me a few details from your dinner last night. You looked amazing in your dress."

"Awe, thanks Mom. It was great. The food was amazing. The atmosphere was great. And there was a guy there that was absolutely gorgeous."

"Gorgeous, huh?" Her mom giggled. "You are a mess girl. What made him so gorgeous?"

"He was tall, handsome, nice to talk to, and a nice dancer."

"Oh, so y'all danced. Is he Spanish?"

"He's Spanish American."

"Interesting. Will you see him again before you leave?"

"Yes, ma'am. We're having dinner tonight at the oldest restaurant in the world."

"Hmm, let me know how it goes. I'm going to try to rest a little before heading out to run errands."

"Yes, please rest. I'll check in with you in a little. I love you."

"I love you, too, Lexie. Send me pics of this restaurant, too."

"Yes, ma'am."

Alexis hung up the phone and decided to Facetime her sister while she had a few minutes to spare. Monica answered quickly.

"Hey baby sis! How is Madrid?"

"Hey Monica. It's great so far. Before we get into all of that have you talked to Mom?"

Monica noticed the concerned look on her sister's face. "I called this morning but she was still in bed. She said she was tired. Have you talked to her?"

"I just got off the phone with her. She didn't sound good, Monica. She sounded exhausted. Said she was about to rest before running a few errands." Alexis shifted on the bed and began to play with one of her loose twists.

"Maybe she's coming down with something. I'll check in with her a few times today. Now, tell me about Spain. That dress you wore last night was gorg…Your ass has gotten fine, too."

Alexis laughed as she looked at her sister's grinning face. She did a head swing from side to side in hopes of swinging her hair and then she smacked her lips. All of this was in agreement with her sister. Honestly, she had been working hard to tone up and it was paying off.

"Thank you. You know I've been working hard. Last night was amazing."

"Give me the deets! You know I'm vicariously living through you right now."

"The restaurant was a vibe. The food was good. But chile, there was a guy there. He was amazing. Just fine as hell."

"Okay, give me his stats."

Alexis rolled her eyes. Only her sister said this to her. "He's 6 '5, handsome, Spanish American, curly hair, gorgeous eyes, muscular or strong back as you like to say. He's intelligent, can hold a conversation and is a great dancer."

"Oh, so y'all out here dancing and shit? Okay, there was a vibe. Please tell me you are seeing him again."

"Yes. In a few minutes. We're having dinner at the oldest restaurant in the world."

"I like the sound of this. But that's what you are wearing?"

"What's wrong with what I have on?" Alexis did a quick twirl for her sister.

"I mean you're dressed like you're headed to Sunday brunch with mom and her church members."

"I am not, Monica." Alexis rolled her eyes.

"Just put on a better-looking shirt. Do you have heels on?"

"Yes, I do Officer Carter."

"I'm not the fashion police. I'm just trying to help you score something."

"Girl, goodbye. I will text you later."

"Go ahead and get off the phone. I know you are about to change shirts, too. Thank me later, lil' girl."

"Bye. I love you."

Alexis hung up the phone before her sister could say anything else. Monica knew her too well. Alexis looked through her clothes and found a less brunchy shirt. In hindsight, Monica was correct. She was dressing "too safe." She found a shirt that hung off her shoulders and paired it with a nice necklace and earring set. She decided to pull her twists up. Of course, she had on her signature red lipstick. If she was being honest, this look was much better than her original look. She snapped a quick picture and sent it to her sister with a quick message.

Alexis: Is this better?

Monica: Of course. Now, have fun and I want to see this amazing looking man.

Alexis: I'll get a picture and send it to you. Love you. Thanks.

Monica: Love you, too, baby girl.

Alexis: Please check on Mom. I'm worried about her.

Monica: Don't be. We got her. Enjoy your much needed vacation.

Alexis sent a heart emoji before she grabbed her purse and a blazer. She headed out her room, to the elevator, and to the lobby. The car would be arriving soon.

CHAPTER THIRTEEN

Alexis waited in the lobby for the private car to pull up. Obviously, this is how Enrique traveled while he was in Spain. In less than five minutes of being in the lobby, the private car pulled up. She knew it was for her once the driver exited. It was the same guy from before.

"Hola, Senor."

"Hola, Senorita."

Alexis slid into the backseat and was surprised to see a dozen red roses. She smiled as the driver smiled at her as well.

"Those are for you, Senorita Carter."

Alexis just nodded and smiled. She grabbed the roses and read the card attached to it.

I'm looking forward to spending another night with you and hopefully dancing more.

- E. Manuel

Alexis was impressed by the penmanship. If this was Enrique's handwriting, it was immaculate. He wrote cursive like they did back in the 18th and 19th centuries. It was very neat. The smile that was plastered on her face made her cheeks hurt. She pulled out her phone and sent Enrique a text message.

Alexis: Thank you so much for the roses. I'm definitely lucky to be spending another night with you as well.

Enrique: I'm the lucky one. Can't wait to see you. Soon.

Alexis: Quick question though. Whose handwriting is on the card?

Enrique: Yours truly. It's one of my hidden talents.

Alexis: It's definitely a lost art these days.

Alexis laid her head back and sighed. This felt so right and so good. She let her mind wander and then she remembered she had access to music. She reached for the iPod and found a Jill Scott playlist. Jill Scott was one of her favorite artists. She loved her sultry, flirty sound.

The car slowed to a stop. She looked up to see Enrique standing outside the restaurant. Alexis took a moment to drink the handsome guy awaiting her arrival. It was short lived as he made the three short steps to open the car door. The smile he wore on his face matched hers.

As much as Alexis was in awe of the hunk of man standing before her, she was even more in awe of the architecture. The attention to detail caught her eye. The bottom half of the restaurant was dark brown wood with lots of small detail. The restaurant's name was placed between the woodwork and the brick work that made up the top. The brick was accessorized with small wrought iron balconies on both sides of double entry doors. The wooden double doors were complimented by windows that allowed for a view inside the restaurant.

Enrique grabbed her hand in his and they headed into the restaurant. She was surprised they skipped much of the seating at the front of the restaurant. Instead, they made their way through the small kitchen where there were little piglets hanging and roasting. The two finally made it back to a small room that housed maybe six tables and were seated in the back corner. There was nothing spectacular about the room. It was cozy, but not what Alexis had in mind. Enrique must have noticed the perplexing look on her face.

"I thought we could skip all the hoopla in the main dining area of the restaurant and enjoy our meal here so we can hear ourselves think and speak."

"Oh, okay because I was definitely wondering why we would dine back here."

"There's usually a lot less fuss back here."

"Right. But why were there piglets hanging and roasting in the kitchen?"

"Don't worry. I have a tour planned for us after we eat. I definitely wouldn't want to do it before and risk you losing your appetite."

"I appreciate that because I really have a weak stomach." Alexis was a picky eater so finding something on the menu that would excite her would be a far stretch. Her excitement was solely based on being at the oldest restaurant in the world. "I think I'll have a half pitcher of sangria and the bread and butter to start," she told Enrique.

"You're having a hard time finding something you like on the menu, huh?"

"Umm, yes. Nothing sounds appealing."

"No worries. We can just have a drink and maybe dessert and we can find something else for dinner. Besides, I would really love to take you to a lounge."

"Sounds good to me. But we are still doing the tour right?"

"Of course. I do need to make a call to ensure we will have dinner when we arrive at our next destination though so I'll do that on the car ride over since we won't be here long."

"Thank you."

Enrique placed their orders and explained to the waitress that they wouldn't actually be dining in. The waitress nodded in understanding and left to place the drink orders and bring some bread and butter back to the table. Which Alexis was very thankful for; she was starving. They made small talk while she drank her sangria and devoured the bread and butter. Occasionally, she would catch Enrique staring with an amused look on his face.

"What?"

"Oh nothing. Just seems like we should skip dessert so I can get you some real food," he said, laughing.

"Yes, because I'm starving."

Soon after, he paid the tab and the tour started. Alexis' body temperature warmed three degrees when Enrique rested his hand at the small of her back as they descended a narrow staircase. They entered a dimly lit room with a lot of things laying around. There were small metal pots, pans, etc. but what stood out the most were the roasters. You could definitely tell they were vintage. Alexis was in awe as she asked lots of questions and caught Enrique grinning at her several times during the tour. She noticed he always stood in close proximity to her and kept his hand touching some part of her body. Not that she cared but it was an observation she made. She could tell that he had very protective instincts. She only recognized them because she noticed the same about her dad and her brother.

Eventually, they made their way back upstairs and did an official tour of the kitchen. Alexis was amazed that the original stove still worked. After the tour, they headed to the car that was waiting for them. Alexis wondered if the driver just sat idly waiting or if Enrique somehow called for them without her noticing. It was very rare for him to be on his phone when they were together, but tonight he pulled his phone out and sent a text message. Less than a minute later, he announced that food would be waiting upon their arrival. He then informed the driver to go to his favorite dance hall. Alexis was interested to see what it looked like because everything and everyone in Madrid seemed so laid back.

They pulled up to a very quaint building that Alexis found to be odd for a dance hall. Enrique exited the car and took the few steps to make it to her side and open her door. She reached for his hand and smiled at the obvious connection between them. He nodded to the driver as they entered the building. There were only a handful of people inside and just as many tables and chairs. Enrique escorted her to a corner table.

The two had barely sat down before a young lady came over and greeted Enrique with a big smile and two to-go containers. Turning to Alexis, Enrique made quick introductions.

"Cecilia, this is Alexis, Alexis, meet my cousin, Cecilia." After they exchanged pleasantries, Cecilia walked away while winking at Enrique. Alexis assumed that was her approval.

She opened her container of food and was surprised to find it filled with pasta and a vegetable medley. It smelled divine and her stomach took that moment to rumble while her mouth began to water. She dug in immediately. Enrique enjoyed his veal, potatoes, and vegetable medley before breaking their comfortable silence.

"I can't wait to dance with you again, Alexis."

"Oh really? So, you liked my dance moves?"

"You did alright but I particularly enjoyed having your body that close to me."

Alexis wasn't expecting such a forthcoming comment. She swept her eyes up from her plate of food and smiled. "I would like that too, Senor Manuel."

"And so, it will be."

That was all the conversation they had while eating dinner. Once they both finished eating, Enrique stood and reached his hand out to Alexis. She obliged.

It was crazy how she fit so comfortably against his body and how it felt so right to be there. Alexis hadn't really paid attention to the music until that moment. It was a soft melody that was designed for slow dancing. They moved to the beat as Enrique sang in her ear. His voice was very throaty and sexy. Surprisingly, he sounded really good.

Being in such close proximity while he sang did something to her senses. Before Alexis knew what she was doing, she leaned back and stood on her tiptoes so her lips could reach his. Alexis expected him to have his eyes closed but he met her gaze head on.

She felt a slight pull and realized Enrique was bringing her body closer to his. Their lips met and magic was made. The magnetic pull was undeniable. The kiss started out slow and sultry and quickly turned passionate as they matched each other's intensity. Enrique and Alexis' tongues mated for what felt like forever. The only reason they broke the kiss was to breathe.

Panting, Alexis tried to back away but her body was prohibited from doing so. Enrique's grip on her waist was forceful yet gentle enough to let her know she was right where he wanted her. And it felt amazing. Alexis looked up at him and smiled. He leaned in and brushed a light kiss across her lips and relinquished just before she could deepen it. The heated look in his eyes told her that was a dangerous game. One that she didn't mind playing.

CHAPTER FOURTEEN

The next morning, Alexis was still on cloud nine. Enrique and she spent the rest of the evening dancing before going back to her hotel. They sat in the hotel lobby engaging in conversation for what felt like hours. He played it safe by not offering to go back to either one of their rooms.

Alexis really hated to leave Madrid and Enrique. However, she was looking forward to the adventures of Barcelona. Her flight was scheduled to depart early that afternoon. She decided to spend the morning with Enrique. They sat quietly in the courtyard of her hotel and enjoyed hot tea. Well, she had hot tea and he enjoyed a cup of coffee. He asked more questions about her siblings and childhood and she did the same for him.

It was interesting learning how he navigated growing up in two different cultures. Of course, his experiences with his mom were a lot different from those when he visited his dad for the summers and holidays. He seemed to have adjusted well. Alexis shared with him how hard of a time she had adjusting after her parents divorced.

"Do you think that has an impact on your relationships?" he asked.

She sat quietly for a moment before responding. "Honestly, I don't think their divorce has had an impact on my relationships. Truthfully, my last relationship would have a far greater impact than my parents' divorce but that's a story for another time. I'll need something stronger than this tea to talk about it."

"Gotcha! So, when was your last relationship?" Alexis let out a deep sigh. Enrique responded. "You don't have to go into details."

"It ended abruptly last year."

"Oh okay. Well, my last serious relationship was about two years ago."

"Serious?" I chuckled. "Were all the other ones not serious or have you just been serial dating?"

"Mainly, just serial dating. The dating pool absolutely sucks. Well, in Austin it does. I have essentially given up for right now. I think anyway…" His words trailed off as he looked out into the courtyard at nothing in particular.

"Yeah, I'm dreading getting back on the dating scene and I'm not sure how long I will delay it. Wanna talk about your last relationship or you need something stronger, too?"

"Nah, I want to keep the playing field even. We can share both of our stories at the same time." He stood and pulled Alexis up and closer to him as he brushed a light kiss across her lips. "I love your hair," he said as he touched her twists. "It reminds me of how my mom wears her hair sometimes."

"Oh really? Do you have a picture of your mom?"

"Of course, I do." He pulled his phone from his pocket and pulled up a picture of his mom. He held it out far enough for Alexis to see.

"She's gorgeous."

And she really was gorgeous. Not at all what Alexis expected. Enrique must look a lot like his dad. His mom had chocolate brown skin, with kinky, coily hair, round eyes, full lips, and very soft facial features. Her hair did look similar, except for the sandy brown color with sprinkles of gray. In the picture, she wore a pink matte lipstick which also surprised Alexis. She looked like she was full of spunk and fun.

"Thank you!"

"You must look a lot like your dad because I really don't see much of your mom in you."

"Yes, I definitely look like my dad but I took my mom's personality. Fun. Adventurous.

Spontaneous. My dad is a planner and drives both Mom and I nuts."

She giggled at his description of his dad's personality. From what Alexis had already learned about Enrique, he was more like his dad than he thought. "Can I see a picture of him?" Enrique showed a picture of his dad. The resemblance was insane. He was a spitting image of his dad. Besides the difference in haircuts and age there were really no recognizable differences. "You two are twins. Just years apart."

"We definitely look alike but we couldn't be any more different."

"Are y'all personalities really that different?"

"Yes, he would do well to take a page out of my book every once in a while. My dad is a great businessman and an even better dad but sometimes all his planning gets in the way of him living his life."

Alexis could hear an unnamed emotion in his voice. Pressing her body a little closer to his, she could feel him smile as he kissed her forehead. He had no idea that forehead kisses were her weakness. It's like they literally zapped all the sense out of her. Being in close proximity to him, she couldn't help but be engulfed in his masculine smell. It was a cedar and musk scent that drove her crazy.

"Okay, let's get you ready to catch your flight. Don't want to make you late to the airport." He grabbed Alexis' hand and interlaced their fingers. She all but swooned at the gesture.

"Oh, I'm not going to be late."

"You will if I continue to hold you in my arms, Alexis."

"...Oh," was all she managed to utter.

Enrique walked Alexis back to her room to grab her suitcases and then headed to the front desk to check out. All she could think about was if this was her last time seeing him. She knew they might exchange text messages from time to time or even call occasionally but was this the last time actually seeing him? Her stomach was in knots. Her steps were a lot slower. If it was her last time seeing him, she wanted to bottle up their last embrace and his forehead kiss.

"Barcelona won't be as fun without me, but I'm sure you will have a great time."

"I was just thinking that. I won't have my personal tour guide, hugger, and kisser."

"Are you saying you like my hugs and kisses, Senorita Carter?"

"Si, Señor Manuel."

His boyish grin made her giggle as he grabbed her luggage to take to the awaiting car. He stopped and pulled Alexis closer to him. He gave her a big hug before leaning in to kiss her senseless. He finally pulled back from the kiss and hugged her again tightly.

It was a relatively short ride to the airport. Enrique held her hand in his for the entire ride, but they didn't say much; both a little sad that their time together had come to an end so quickly. Once they arrived at the airport, Enrique grabbed her bags and headed inside. He pulled her into him and instinctively, she leaned in for a kiss, a goodbye kiss. The passion in the kiss was amazing. He didn't rush and Alexis didn't feel a need to rush either. When they both pulled back for air, Alexis noticed a small crowd that was watching intently.

"I think we put on a great show," she whispered.

"This wasn't even the beginning. We can give them a show if that's what they need this morning."

"Umm, it's not what I need."

"I'm joking," he said, showing off his gorgeous smile. "But hey, my gorgeous brown skin girl, we will definitely keep in touch. I have a lot more hugs and forehead kisses for you.”

Alexis’ weak smile was hopeful, yet anxious. She wanted to know how he planned to make that happen living in two different states. Grabbing her luggage, Alexis headed towards security. Enrique took the few steps to close the gap between them. Turning back, Alexis looked at him and he smiled.

“Sooner than you think, Alexis.”

CHAPTER FIFTEEN

The flight to Barcelona was short. By the time she had gotten comfortable enough to take a nap, the pilot made the announcement that they were making the final descent.

After a much-needed nap in her new room, Alexis went in search of food. She would relax and chill today but tomorrow she planned to have a little fun. The first adventure would be the subway. She hadn't had great experiences with public transportation but was willing to try it. The plan was to go to the City Centre and explore different shops and activities.

Alexis hadn't realized that her phone notifications were on do not disturb. She had a few missed calls from her mom, sister, and Enrique. There were also text messages from them as well as Reign and Brooklyn. She responded to the texts from her mom and sister first.

She decided to FaceTime group chat with Monica, Reign, and Brooklyn. Surprisingly, all three answered and were available to talk. They chatted for about twenty minutes while she enjoyed a sandwich from the hotel's deli. Once she ended her call with them, Alexis sent Enrique a text message.

Alexis: Hey, I see I missed your call and text messages. What's up?

Enrique: You are what's up. I was worried about you. How was your flight?

Alexis: Worried, why? The flight was quick. I didn't even get to take my nap.

Enrique: Worried because I can. Did you get some rest?

Alexis: Yes. I just finished grabbing a bite to eat. I'm just going to relax and chill today. Tomorrow I'll find some adventure.

Enrique: What are you thinking about doing tomorrow? You need some suggestions?

Alexis: Tomorrow is the day that I try out the subway. I plan to go to a mall and do some shopping. I'll have to find a fancy restaurant. You have given me plenty of suggestions. But what else do you suggest?

Enrique: I suggest you travel outside the city. You will love the smaller villages but there is plenty to do in the city.

Enrique provided a lot more options and Alexis felt like she had enough for the week. However, she just knew she wasn't going outside the city. No way.

The next two days went by quickly. The subway wasn't too horrible of an experience. Alexis did get on the wrong train trying to get back to the hotel but luckily, she spoke just enough broken Spanish to get the help that she needed.

Most of her third day was spent at the City Centre. There was so much to see and do. She texted Enrique randomly throughout the day and he made sure to call before it got too late. They didn't spend a lot of time on the phone. Although she was enjoying her time in Barcelona, Alexis had to admit that she really did miss him. They had just gotten off the phone when her text messages dinged.

Enrique: I miss you, gorgeous brown skin girl.

Alexis: I was just thinking how I miss you, too.

Enrique: You want some company in Barcelona?

Alexis: Umm, yes but don't rearrange your schedule for me though.

Enrique: I'll see you tomorrow. It'll be fun and adventurous.

Alexis: Really? I can't wait.

Enrique: Me either. Good night, Alexis.

Alexis: Buenas noches, Señor Manuel.

The smile Alexis wore was crazy big. Enrique was going to join her in Barcelona. She couldn't wait to spend more time with him.

Alexis was giddy as hell the next day. She still couldn't believe Enrique was joining her in Barcelona. Although they had spoken on the phone every day since she left Madrid, she couldn't wait to be in his presence. Quite honestly, she was dying to share another kiss with him. He left his mark on her four days ago.

She spent a lot of her time daydreaming about the kiss they shared. Well kisses because there had been more than one. The heat that surged through her body was like no other. The electric current that took charge over her desires was intense. It had taken all her willpower not to undress and have her way with him. She couldn't promise that would be the case once he arrived in a few hours.

Alexis continued to get dressed for the day. Enrique informed her that he had a full agenda for them once he arrived and she couldn't wait. The temperatures were mild. Not too hot or too cold, so she put on jeans and a thin, long sleeve shirt with her chucks. She always had her chucks with her. The first three days were relaxing with a little sightseeing. The next few days would be fun filled before she headed back to Atlanta.

Alexis frowned at the thought of heading back. Not because she didn't want to get back home but because she wondered where that would leave her and Enrique.

As life would have it, I met someone I'm vibing with while on vacation in Spain. Alexis giggled at her luck. Shaking her head, she grabbed her phone to send a quick message to Reign and Brooklyn. Dressed, she left her room and headed downstairs to grab breakfast.

Alexis enjoyed pancakes, potatoes, fruit, and fruit juice for breakfast. She sat in the dining area and people watched. There were so many people and so much interaction, especially for this small boutique hotel. One younger couple in particular caught her attention. The young man was so attentive and the young lady was very appreciative. Alexis was captivated by how the young man catered to his lady. A fleeting thought of Remington crossed her mind. One of the things she learned in therapy was to think of Remington in his totality and not just the bad that took place. She also knew it was okay for her to reminisce on the fond memories that they shared. She always enjoyed how he catered to her when he didn't have his head down working.

He could be very attentive yet the attention she received from Enrique seemed more genuine. Maybe because she now knew Remington was being deceitful. The attention felt different with Enrique. He hadn't known her long but was going to great lengths to spend time with her. Him taking time away from his family was a big deal to her. She said multiple times that he didn't have to yet he insisted on spending more time with her before she headed back to Atlanta. Alexis smiled at the thought.

Time had gone by so fast. She left the dining area and headed back to her room. She and Enrique would not be sharing a room but he booked a room at the same hotel. She knew he could have easily stayed at one of his family's short-term rental properties but he didn't. If she was being honest, she was longing to stand flushed against his 6'5 frame and to have his long fingers caress her hand and his lips touch her lips. She was ready to see him like she hadn't seen him in months.

As soon as Alexis stepped into her room, she received a text from Enrqiue.

Enrique: Senorita Carter…I just landed. I'll have a car bring me to the hotel. Let's link up in about an hour.

Alexis: Hola Senor Manuel. That works for me. See you then. *kisses*

Enrique: Oh, so you want to kiss me again?

Alexis: Absolutely.

Enrique: I love your honesty. I'll make sure you get what you want.

Alexis: I'll hold you to that.

Enrique: As you should.

Alexis: Stop flirting with me. It's a dangerous game.

Enrique: It's not a game and I plan to show you. See you soon.

Alexis giggled while the biggest grin took over her face. Flirting was her thing. Always had been, so she wasn't concerned. What wasn't her thing was trying to avoid Enrique getting into her system. She already couldn't stop thinking about the kisses they shared. She took a seat in the chair facing the balcony of her room and pulled out her journal from her backpack next to the chair. Her desire to write was intense.

What are the odds of me meeting a fine ass man while on vacation? We are a whole vibe together. We laugh. We have fun and it's a feeling I haven't felt in a while. He's an amazing kisser. And kissing is my thing as long as the person can kiss. I'm wondering what happens when I leave Spain. Do we send the occasional text message or make the out of the blue phone calls? Atlanta and Austin are a lot closer than Atlanta and

Spain yet both are so far away. I just know when I leave here, I'm going to miss him. I wonder how long it will take me to get him out of my system. I plan to get as many kisses as possible before I leave.

– ACarter

Alexis closed her journal and closed her eyes. Taking deep breaths, she decided not to get too far ahead with her thinking. Being present in the moment was important for her. It wasn't easy but it always helped to alleviate her anxiety. Not sure how long she had been sitting there with her eyes closed, her phone beeped indicating she had a text message. It was Enrique.

Enrique: I'm downstairs in the lobby. What's your room number and I'll head up.

Alexis: 7G

Enrique: Okay, I'm headed to you.

Alexis' excitement was overwhelming. She needed to get herself together. Less than three minutes later there was a knock on her door. Alexis opened the door to find Enrique standing there with a bouquet of roses. Mostly yellow and a few red roses.

"Enrique, these are beautiful. Thank you."

"You are welcome. Now, come here."

Holding the bouquet in one hand and pulling Alexis closer to his body with his other, Enrique brushed his lips across Alexis' lips. A hunger and desire took over Alexis. She deepened the kiss and Enrique matched her energy. They both pulled back to breath and Alexis saw the heat in his eyes. He stepped into the room, walked to the side table by her bed, and sat the bouquet on the table.

Alexis opened her mouth to say something but he captured her thought with his mouth. The kiss was intense and mesmerizing. Alexis pulled back first this time. She ran her index finger across her lips. She looked up to see Enrique staring at her with a sly grin.

"Do you still think it's a game, senorita?"

"Not at all, senor."

He smirked. "Good, let's get ready to have some fun. Oh, just so you know there's more where that came from."

"Oh really. Will it be rationed out?"

"Nope, you can have as much of it as you like. Whenever. Wherever."

"Noted. What's the plan for today?"

"I have a few places for us to visit. Then tomorrow we will head to a small Spanish village, Baga, and we will also visit Ax-les-

Thermes in Italy. The next day we will visit Andorra. Are you familiar with that country?"

"No, it sounds fun though. I can't wait. What's the plan for the last day?"

"We'll chill and enjoy each other's company while we figure out how we'll keep in touch after Spain."

"Oh, okay. I like that idea. Ready?"

"Whenever you are." Alexis and Enrique left her room and headed downstairs. Of course, Enrique had a car waiting for them. "I figured we could go sightseeing in some of the neighborhoods off the beaten paths. I also want to show you a building my mom helped design."

Alexis could barely contain her excitement. "Oh cool. I can't wait to see it."

CHAPTER SIXTEEN

The next day, Alexis was up earlier than usual. The drive to Baga, Spain was about an hour and half. This would be the first time Enrique would be driving and not utilizing his car service. Alexis dressed comfortably in her New Balance running shoes, denim shorts, and t-shirt declaring the future is female and black. She added her crossbody to her attire and was ready to go. Before she made her way downstairs, she sent a text to her mom.

Alexis: Hi Mom. I know it's late but I hope you are feeling better. Call me in the morning.

Unexpectedly, Alexis received an immediate response from her mom.

Mom: Hey baby! I'm restless tonight so I've been up reading. I hope you are having fun. What time is it there?

Alexis: Do you feel better? It's a little after 8 AM here.

Mom: Oh, why are you up so early? What are your plans for the day?

Alexis noticed her mom was avoiding her question.

Alexis: Headed to a small village in Spain…Baga. It's about an hour and half away.

Mom: Are you going alone or with a group?

Alexis: Enrique and I are driving up to the village.

Mom: Oh really? So, he followed you to Barcelona?

Alexis: LOL! No, he didn't follow me. He decided to come visit my last few days here.

Mom: Okay, have fun and don't worry about me. I'm fine.

Alexis: Okay. I love you and I'll call you later today. Get some rest.

Mom: I will. I love you too, baby girl.

Alexis exhaled loudly. She knew her mom well enough to know she wasn't being honest about how she felt. Parents could be so frustrating sometimes but she also understood her mom didn't want her or her siblings to be worried. Alexis fumbled with her crossbody purse and headed downstairs. She stood in the lobby waiting for Enrique to make his grand entrance and she for sure knew it would be grand.

Unfortunately, there was somewhat of a crowd downstairs that morning. However, she couldn't wait to see his handsome, smiling face. Maybe that would put her in a better mood. She was worried about her mom but there wasn't much she could do halfway around the world. She would definitely be making a trip home when she returned from vacation.

While Alexis stood looking out into the courtyard, she was brought out of her trance when she felt a hand at her waist. She didn't have to turn to know it was Enrique, the electric charge she felt told her as much.

"Good morning, Ms. Carter." Alexis closed her eyes as the sound of his voice consumed her.

"Good morning, Mr. Manuel."

"Did you sleep well?"

"Yes," she nodded. "Did you?"

"Could have slept better."

"Why? Was your room not comfortable?"

"It had nothing to do with my room. I missed your company."

"Oh."

That was all Alexis could utter. Enrique turned her around just in time to see she was blushing. He gave her wink and leaned in to brush a quick kiss across her lips.

"That's a proper good morning greeting. Hell, a proper greeting altogether. You ready?"

"Yes, I'm ready. And thanks for properly greeting me."

"Of course, anytime."

Enrique and Alexis stepped out the lobby doors holding hands and were greeted by the valet driver. Enrique opened the passenger door to a black Cadillac Escalade. *Of course, he would have an SUV for his long ass legs,* Alexis thought. He gracefully walked to the other side and got into the driver's seat. He made some adjustments to the seats and mirrors and they were on their way. Alexis used this time to steal glimpses of Enrique as he focused on the road.

She noticed his strong jawline and how it occasionally flexed. She also noticed how his masculine scent took over her sense of smell; she couldn't smell anything else in his presence. She particularly loved watching his thigh muscles flex under his jeans when he made the necessary movements to press the gas or hit the brakes. It was all enticing and almost overwhelming in the best way possible.

Baga was nestled in the Pyrenees Mountain. Alexis was mesmerized by the cobblestone streets and colorful architecture. Even more impressive was the natural landscape of the small town. The streets were almost deserted but there were a few folks here and there. Their first stop was at a pastry shop that Enrique spoke very highly of.

The pastries did not disappoint. They were light and airy yet very tasty. The next stop was the historic church of Baga. From there the two navigated the winding roads that lead to more houses in the small village and eventually were at the medieval center. Enrique gave what little facts he could about the village. Alexis appreciated his effort and enjoyed learning. He was just as intrigued as she was. The amusement in his eyes was also reflected in hers. Alexis grabbed his hand and they walked hand in hand down the cobblestone streets.

They continued to hold hands as they made their way back to the car. It was then that she had the strongest urge to feel his lips. Alexis leaned in and stood on her tiptoes. "Kiss me," she whispered.

"Of course, my brown skin girl."

And boy did he kiss her. It was even more mind blowing than the previous kisses they shared. It was so amazing that Alexis didn't want to come up for air. Thank goodness for Enrique's good sense because she had no intention of breaking the kiss. He was a lot more sensible. He stood staring at her as he gently ran his thumb across her lips. A small smile touched his lips.

"You are amazing, Alexis. Come on, let's head to our next destination."

"What's our next destination?" She asked as they got into the car.

"We'll make a short drive over the border to France and visit the spa town. So, I hope you are up for a spa day."

"Of course, I am. What girl wouldn't be?"

He winked as he continued to drive out of the parking lot. "Feel free to connect your Bluetooth and play whatever music you like. I usually ride in silence."

"We can definitely ride in silence then. I don't want your concentration broken while driving through these mountains."

"Baby, I'm an expert driver in all terrain and weather. Remember that, okay?"

"Whatever, Enrique."

Alexis sat back and pulled her phone from her purse. She sent a quick text to her mom with a few of the pictures. Then she opened her Kindle app and started reading a book she started a few days ago. Life felt so great with Enrique.

When Alexis was with Enrique she felt more relaxed. He definitely felt familiar and comfortable but she also felt safe and secure. Safe and secure from physical harm but his presence brought her a peace of mind, too. She felt emotionally safe. They also had fun together. She loved how he was so attentive to her and went above and beyond to make sure her needs and wants were met. Another fleeting thought of Remington crossed her mind. She really couldn't compare the two.

Ax-les-Thermes is a small mountain town located in France near the Spanish border and not far from Andorra. The town was known for its spas and various outdoor activities. They walked through town and enjoyed the mountainous views as well as the river that ran through the center. At the spa, they both began with a thirty-minute facial and then a ninety-minute massage. Following the massage, they grabbed a bite to eat at a small café before trying their luck at the casino in town.

"Hey, are you okay with staying overnight at our next destination and exploring it tomorrow?" Enrique asked.

"Umm, what's the next destination? You've done enough driving for the day."

"Next, we are headed to the perfume capital of the world."

"Huh? That's really a thing?"

"Yes, you haven't heard of it?"

"Umm, no. Are you joking because I love perfume!"

"Not at all. Andorra is also known as the perfume capital of the world."

"Oh, wow I've never heard of that country. How far away is it?"

"It's about an hour drive from here but it's about three hours from Barcelona. So, instead of driving back in the morning, I figured we could stay overnight, enjoy the day there, and head back around mid-day.

"Sounds like a plan to me. All of this has been a great plan but I don't have an overnight bag or anything."

"Of course, we can stop at one of the local stores before heading to Andorra."

"I should've known you thought about it all."

"Yes, I did. Now come let me kiss you."

Alexis giggled and obliged his request.

They made a few stops at different stores and finally arrived in Andorra a little before seven o'clock. Enrique and Alexis decided that sharing a room would be fine. They also decided to order room service. She was thankful that the hotel had a laundry area because she needed to wash the clothes she had just purchased. She did that while Enrique ordered room service.

They spent the rest of the night talking about everything and the topic of relationships came back around. Alexis gave him a high-level explanation of the shit show that was her engagement night. He sat in disbelief that anyone could be so damn selfish. Alexis was particularly proud of herself because she didn't feel the same angst or pain telling Enrique how things went down. Therapy was definitely working.

"Hey, come here, my brown skin girl." Alexis took Enrique's outstretched hand, relaxing her body against his. "I'm sorry your ex didn't value what he had in you. You deserved more than he was willing to give."

"I know. It wasn't easy to heal from but I did and for that I'm grateful. It could have easily broken me."

He placed a kiss on her forehead and eventually made his way to her lips. Alexis' soul smiled at his gentle yet masculine presence.

"Let's get some rest. We have a fun-filled day ahead of us tomorrow. I can't wait for you to enjoy the perfume capital."

"Yes, let's get some rest."

As hesitant as Alexis was to share a bed with Enrique, she was also equally excited about having the masculine feel of him next to her. Kissing was definitely as far as she wanted to take it at the moment, but it had been a while since she had been held by a man. Honestly, she craved that at the moment and she knew Enrique would give her just what she needed. They snuggled in close with Enrique's arm thrown over Alexis' waist. His musky scent enveloped her and she smiled. "Good night, Senor Manuel."

"Good night, Senorita Carter."

Alexis was asleep before she knew it. She slept soundly through the night and was awakened when the warmth of Enrique's body disappeared. She rolled onto her side to see exactly where he was and saw him sitting in the bedside chair staring intently at her. A smile touched his lips as soon as she fluttered her eyes open completely.

"Good morning, sleepy head."

"Good morning, Enrique. Why are you awake so early?"

"It's not early. It's almost 10 o'clock. You seemed pretty tired, so I decided you needed to sleep."

"Oh, my goodness. I'm sorry. I didn't realize it was this late. I know you wanted to get started early today."

"Calm down, Alexis. It's not that big of a deal. We don't have a set itinerary so we can move at our own pace. Hot tea?"

"Umm, yes. I'll get dressed while it's steeping."

Enrique pulled his long physique from the chair and headed toward the countertop in the kitchenette. Pulling out a teacup, a tea kettle, and tea, he began preparation for Alexis' morning pick me up. Alexis went into the restroom and began her morning routine. She really preferred to start her morning with a cup of room temperature water first but she would have to be very intentional about drinking plenty of water throughout the day.

She flossed and brushed her teeth, rinsed with mouthwash, and then cleansed her face before moisturizing. She grabbed the yoga pants, t-shirt, and sports bra from the dresser top and dressed quickly. She shook her twists and just like that she was ready to head out. Enrique stood in the kitchenette pouring honey into her tea.

"Here you are, madam," he said, handing her the cup of tea.

"Thank you! Give me about five minutes to drink this tea and I'll be ready for today's adventures."

"Sure thing," he said as he placed a kiss on her forehead. He had no idea he was killing her with the forehead kisses. She started humming, *Killing Me Softly*, by Lauren Hill.

The day was amazing. They visited several perfume shopping centers. Why anyone would need fragrance shops to be open twenty-four hours was beyond anything Alexis could fathom. But she was a lover of fragrances so her excitement got the best of her. She bought so many bottles of perfumes and colognes.

They decided on a quick lunch before exploring what else Andorra had to offer besides the massive collection of fragrances. Soon after, they started the three-hour drive back to Barcelona. Reality set in for Alexis, she only had one more full day to spend with Enrique and then they would go back to their separate lives.

"Do we have anything planned for tomorrow?" Alexis asked.

"I figured we could just chill and plan how to continue seeing each other once we return to the states. I mean if that's what you want to do?"

"Of course, I would love that."

They both rode in silence, each with a content look on their face. Alexis started her playlist but she eventually fell asleep.

Enrique appreciated the fact that he could steal glimpses while she slept. He knew that her chocolate brown skin, kinky hair, radiant smile, and curious eyes would forever be etched into his memory. She was the most beautiful woman he had ever kissed. Hell, the most beautiful woman he had ever laid his eyes on. It wasn't just her looks but her fun, adventurous spirit, intelligence, and genuine personality. He was mesmerized by her and he planned to make sure they continued to experience what they had at the moment.

"Can I ask you something," Enrique asked once she'd woken up.

"Of course. What's up?"

"How do you see this working once we get back to the states?" he questioned. "I mean I know how I want it to work but I want your thoughts."

"Umm, I don't know. I guess it will mean a lot of traveling back and forth when we have time."

"We will make time. I know for sure I will make time."

She smiled at his intentions. "I can definitely make time, too." Alexis fidgeted with her twists. Was she really ready to be in a relationship, more importantly a long-distance relationship? "What's the worst-case scenario for us?"

"Umm, worst case scenario is we can't make the long-distance work. We know we have chemistry, Alexis."

"I know but I don't want to waste each other's time. Relationships are hard already and distance will make it that much harder."

"Relationships are not hard. Relationships are fun. We will keep our vibe that we've had in Spain." Alexis was getting ready to object when Enrique continued, "Hear me out. I'm not saying it won't have challenges but I'm making a promise to you to overcome whatever challenges we may face." He could tell that Alexis was hesitant but he also knew she felt the same chemistry he felt. He grabbed her hands and held them as he looked into her eyes. "You have to trust me, Alexis. You will find out soon enough I make things happen for the people that are important in my life. And I have no reason to believe that you won't be one of those people."

"Okay, I'll trust you and I can make time."

He didn't see the smile that he had grown accustomed to seeing which let him know she was still uncertain about the terms.

"I can show you better than I can tell you but if at any time you aren't feeling the arrangement let me know. Open, honest communication is very important and it will be paramount in a long-distance relationship."

CHAPTER seventeen

Alexis didn't get much sleep the night before, so she was up earlier than usual. While it was reassuring that she and Enrique would make time for each other, she hated the thought of leaving him. It sounded crazy but she really wanted to spend a few more weeks, months, or years in their little bubble. It was so peaceful and it felt good to be surrounded by his masculine peace.

Alexis' bags were packed and she was dreading the drive to the airport, the flight back, and time away from Enrique. Everything was moving in slow motion, except for time. Before she knew it, it was time to head to the airport.

The flight seemed a lot longer and sleep did not find her. By the time she landed in Atlanta, she could hardly keep her eyes open. Thank goodness for global entry. The customs line was insanely long and she knew for a fact that she wouldn't have made it standing in line. It was so bittersweet to be home. She missed her house but she missed Enrique even more. Alexis let out a sigh. She would have a lot to unpack in her next therapy session because as crazy as it sounded, she really could feel herself falling in love with Enrique. It had to be the lack of sleep.

She was so drained that she had forgotten to turn her phone back on once she landed in Atlanta. Once she made it through customs, she turned it on and her notifications went crazy. Everyone knew when her flight got in so she wondered why she had so many messages. *What the hell is going on?*

Alexis started going through them and most of them were from her siblings. There were a few from Reign and Brooklyn saying they would pick her up. Alexis started reading messages in her sibling group chat and her heart sank. *Oh no. Momma has to be okay.*

She pulled her phone out to order her Uber but before she could, Brooklyn was calling her.

"Hey Lexie, we are here at the airport to pick you up. Are you okay?"

"Umm, yes. I just need to get home so I can get to my mom as soon as possible."

"We know. That's why we are here."

"Okay, I'll be coming out soon."

"Are you sure you're okay?" Reign asked.

"Yes, I think so."

As soon as Alexis walked out the door, Brooklyn and Reign were there waiting for her. Reign hopped out and assisted Alexis with putting her bags in the trunk. She gave Alexis a big, tight hug but didn't say anything. If anyone knew her, it was these two. They knew when to push her but they also knew when to give her space. That was the benefit of years of friendships. She couldn't appreciate them any more than what she did at this moment. She needed time to think. She sent a quick text message to the sibling group text.

Alexis: I just landed in Atlanta. I'll be heading to Memphis soon. How is Mom?

Monica: Maybe you should rest a day or two, Lexie. She is okay. She's stable. No changes. Heavily sedated.

Eric: Yes, Lexie. Give yourself a day or two to rest.

Alexis: No, I want to be there with her. With y'all.

She didn't get anything back from the group text. Alexis laid her head against the back of the seat. "Thank you both so much for picking me up and making sure I was okay. I appreciate it."

"Of course," they said in unison.

Alexis' voice cracked. All the emotions of her mom being in the hospital, having to leave Enrique and trying to sort through the emotions attached to him were starting to be too much. She already missed him but she felt terrible for even thinking about him at the moment. Her mom was gravely ill and she was thinking about somebody's son. But he wasn't just somebody's son to her. She probably should let him know what was going on with her mom. She was brought out of her trance when she heard Brooke ask her something.

"I'm sorry. I was lost in my thoughts. What did you say?"

"What's your plan? Will you be heading to Memphis today?"

"Eric and Monica seem to think I should take a day or two to rest but I'm sure I won't be getting any rest. Maybe I'll just fly out. Get a one-way ticket."

"Umm, a day to recoup and get yourself together may not be that bad," Reign said.

"I agree with Reign."

"And I honestly can't believe you two are agreeing on something. I'll see how I feel and I'll also check flights. It may make sense for me to drive though."

"Why? You can always drive one of Moncia's cars," Brook responded.

"Right."

Alexis decided to text Enrique.

Alexis: Made it to Atlanta safely. I'll be headed to Memphis tonight or first thing in the morning. My mom is in the hospital and isn't doing too well.

A couple of minutes went by and she hadn't received a response from Enrique. She felt a tinge of disappointment which was crazy. There was a time difference and he had a life. She closed her eyes as they pulled into her subdivision. Just as Brooke was pulling into her driveway, her phone rang.

"Hello?"

"Hey, Alexis. I just got your message," Enrique said. "What's going on?"

"Umm, I don't know all the details. I just know she isn't doing well. So, I'm going to head to Memphis for a few days or weeks."

"Okay, what do you need from me? What can I do?"

"Nothing, Enrique. I just wanted to let you know what was going on."

"Are you sure you don't need anything?"

"Positive. Can I call you back once I'm in the house and settled? We just pulled into my driveway."

"Of course, baby. Call me back when you feel like talking."

"Okay, talk to you later, bye." Alexis hung up the phone and noticed the two pairs of eyes on her. "What?" she asked, rolling her eyes.

"Nothing," Reign said.

"Nothing? Nah, we have questions," Brooke responded.

"Not now, Brooke," Reign replied.

"Right, but later."

After retrieving her bags from the car, Alexis headed inside. She was relieved to be home but knew it would be short lived. She immediately pulled out her laptop and started looking up flights. Of course, the prices were crazy expensive but she was fine with it. She needed to make sure she didn't have any in-person client meetings. After checking both calendars, she booked a flight for first thing the next morning.

Reign and Brooklyn hung around for a few. Soon after they left she sent a text message to Enrique to see if he was free to talk. He called immediately.

"Hey Alexis. How are you?"

"I'm okay. You're up late."

"I was waiting for you to call. How's your mom?"

"No change. I'll be there tomorrow morning."

"Oh okay. Glad you decided to wait until morning. Do you need anything from me?"

"No," she said while getting comfortable. "Hearing your voice is enough."

There was a pause. Alexis didn't really know what to make of the silence but Enrique didn't let it linger for too long. "I'm happy I can provide some comfort. Even though I'm halfway around the world. I wish I were closer."

"Me too."

Alexis was surprised by the vulnerability she was showing. It could be the emotions of not knowing what's going on with her mom or the fact Enrique wasn't physically close. Or it could be because she was just that comfortable with him. Which seemed a little premature since she had only met him two weeks ago.

"I'll make sure I get to Atlanta when I get back. I head back to the states at the end of the week. Maybe the following weekend I can come out there."

Alexis sighed at the thought of being in his arms again, "That would be great. Well, it depends on Mom. I'll be there until I'm comfortable coming back to Atlanta. Sorry, it's so up in the air."

"Hey. No need to apologize. I understand. I wouldn't want to leave my mom either."

"Yeah. So, what have you been up to?"

"Honestly, nothing. Helping my dad and uncle with a few things. I had a lot more fun when you were here."

"I really miss Spain. I miss you, too. Thank you for showing me an amazing time."

"Of course, my brown skin girl. There's more to come."

The emphasis on *my* wasn't lost on Alexis. It actually made her smile.

"I like the sound of that."

"I'll let you get some rest. I know you have an early morning. Will you let me know when you make it to Memphis?"

"Of course, I will. Thanks for caring. I appreciate you."

"You have no idea. Rest up and I'll text you later but if you need to talk before then I'm available anytime."

"Thank you. Good night, Senor Manuel."

"Buenas noches, Señorita Carter."

Alexis knew she wasn't sleepy but she didn't want to hold Enrique on the phone. It was almost 2 AM in Spain so she knew he was probably tired. It felt like things were moving so fast with them. She knew the distance would definitely cause things to slow down. She mustered enough energy to pack a bag for tomorrow. She had to be at the airport no later than 5:30 AM and she was depending on Reign. Hopefully, she wouldn't regret it. Her ass was never on time for anything but she was insistent on taking Alexis to the airport.

Sleep was the last thing on her mind. She was worried about her mom while also trying to figure out what was happening between her and Enrique. Writing was her thing yet she couldn't manage to get anything on paper. With all the thoughts taking up space in her brain, nothing made sense when she tried to put it on paper. Alexis started to do things around the house, starting in her office. She still had a lot to organize in there and this was the perfect time to do so. She worked until she lost track of time. She heard her phone ding in the other room.

Enrique: Good morning, my brown skin girl. Have a safe flight. Let me know when you make it.

Alexis smiled a big goofy grin. She didn't know what was happening with them but she made a promise to herself to just enjoy it. He was definitely bringing her joy when she needed it most.

Alexis: Good morning, handsome. Thank you and I will. Believe it or not, I haven't been to sleep. I'm about to shower, get dressed, and wait on Reign to pick me up for the airport.

Enrique: I know you must be exhausted. Please try to get some rest once you get to Memphis. You know you could have called me, too?

Alexis: I was not about to disturb your sleep, Enrique.

Enrique: Alexis, you disturbed my sleep the moment I saw you walk into that restaurant more than two weeks ago. So, I would've been fine.

Her shoulders relaxed. She hadn't noticed how tense she was but Enrique was giving her comfort even from halfway around the world. This long-distance thing may not be that bad after all. She would trust him. Trust them. Live in the moment. *Okay, Lord. I'll live in the moment. Well, Lord and Ms. Juanita, because I know she will appreciate me living in the moment, too.*

Alexis: Awe, that's cute. Lil' smooth talking self.

Enrique: I mean, I am smooth but I'm telling the truth.

Alexis: *blushing* I'll call you once I make it to the airport.

Enrique: I can't wait to hear your voice.

Alexis took a seat on the edge of her bed. Enrique was her light in this dark moment. Her mind slowly traveled to her mom who is usually so vibrant and full of life. She didn't want to imagine her not living the life she created for herself. The divorce was tough on her mom and Alexis witnessed her putting her life back together after a twenty-six-year marriage. It wasn't easy but her mom was intentional about creating happiness. So, why had she neglected her health? *I just hope she'll be okay.* Finally, Alexis got up and headed into the bathroom to shower.

After her quick shower, she sent a text to Reign to make sure she was on her way.

Alexis: Hey Reign bow! Good morning. Are you on your way?

Reign: I just pulled into your driveway.

Alexis: Wait, what? You're early.

Reign: Girl, hush. I'm coming in through the garage.

Alexis: Okay.

Reign let herself in and made her way upstairs. Alexis was happy to be dressed because her friends had no boundaries. They would just barge into the bedroom with not so much as a tap on the damn door.

"Hey girl. How are you feeling this morning?" Reign asked.

"I'm fine. Just tired as hell and ready to see what's going on with Momma."

"She will be fine. She's definitely a fighter. That's all I've ever known Ms. Carter to be."

"A fighter and feisty as hell. Why were you up so early?"

"Because I didn't want to hear your damn mouth if I was late."

They both started laughing. Everyone knew Reign was notorious for being late. She was never on time for anything. Alexis dreaded the day she got married. She knew it would start hours late on account of her.

"Well, okay. Let's get me to the airport on time, too."

"You bet." Reign grabbed a bag and Alexis grabbed the roller suitcase. She hadn't realized how much she packed until she lifted the bag to carry it downstairs. "You think you packed enough?"

"Shit, too much as usual."

The drive to the airport was a short ride. They spoke briefly about Enrique and the telephone conversation earlier.

"Oh, he likes you. It's exciting but how are you feeling about it?"

"Excited. Nervous. You know my track record isn't that great."

"No, I know Remington sold you a pipe dream. That's on him. Not you."

"Right."

"You sound like you need convincing. Alexis, you are an amazing human being which means you are, were, and will be an amazing girlfriend and everything beyond that, too."

"I know. It just feels fast but it does feel right. Too right almost."

"Go with the flow. You'll be fine. What's meant to be will be."

"But how are you?"

"Girl, I'm okay. I literally take things one day at a time. Life is better that way."

"I know. I can't wait to come back and start our shenanigans back up."

"I know. It's been a while since we last hung out. Even Justice is ready to get out the house."

"What? Momma Justice is ready to leave paradise and join the likes of our heathen asses?"

"Girl, yes. Let's do brunch at my house when you get back. All four of us."

"Your brunches get a little wild. So, yes. Might be what we all need."

Pulling up to the airport, they hugged and Alexis grabbed her bags out of the truck. The Atlanta airport was always busy and she hoped the TSA pre-check line wasn't as long as the general boarding line. Sometimes, it just defeats the purpose of having pre-check. Thankfully, it moved pretty quickly. Once she got through security and made her way to her gate, she texted Enrique to see if he was busy.

Alexis: Are you busy? I made it to my gate at the airport.

Enrique: Never too busy for you.

Her phone started ringing before she could call him.

"Good morning, Alexis."

"Good afternoon. How's your day been so far?"

"Not bad. I'm going to head to the restaurant a little later to help out."

"Oh, how's that been going?"

"We've been busy and the restaurant is a little understaffed right now so I never know what task I'll be assigned. Last night, I was waiting tables. I would much rather hand wash dishes."

Alexis giggled. "Was it that bad?"

"Yes, it was."

"I would've loved for you to be my server. Would've been such a pleasant view."

"Can you imagine my tall self walking up to your table asking for your drink and dinner order?"

"It would have been a little different but I would've enjoyed looking at you. Wait, that means other women are enjoying looking at you, too." Alexis said it in a joking manner but there was a tinge of jealousy. She needed to get a therapy session because she was officially losing her mind. But why did it feel so good to be this way with him?

"What's your plan when you get to Memphis? Are you going directly to the hospital or will you go to your mom's house first?"

"I'll probably go to Momma's first and drop by bags. Don't really want them in my sister's car like that."

"Oh yea, that makes sense. Let me know what hospital your mom is in so I can send flowers."

"Awe, that's sweet. I'll text you the hospital, address, and her room number when I get there."

"Okay. Safe travels. Hey, try not to worry too much and remember I'm only a phone call or text message away."

"I know. Thank you. I'll talk to you later."

"Okay, bye."

CHAPTER EIGHTEEN

The next few days were crazy busy. Alexis hadn't known what to expect when she got to the hospital but seeing her mom laid up in the bed was very disheartening. She was happy that she was making progress and she was scheduled for surgery in two days. Turns out she had a few different issues. She was being tested for ovarian and endometrial cancers. Just hearing the word cancer was scary. The doctors would perform a hysterectomy and what they saw would determine if it would be a full or partial.

Right now, it was just a waiting game to get her stabilized and feeling better before surgery. Enrique kept his promise and sent her a beautiful bouquet of assorted flowers. She was in a lot of pain but she managed to smile really big when she got them. She had always been a flower girl. Alexis made a mental note to send her more.

It was the day of her mom's surgery and Alexis was a ball of nerves. She was more nervous than her mom. She hadn't spoken to Enrique since the night before. She'd called his phone but it went straight to voicemail and he hadn't responded to any of her text messages. He wasn't scheduled to fly back to the states for another three or four days. She hoped everything was okay.

The last thing she needed to do was be worried about him and her mom. So, she decided to focus her energy on her mom. Maybe Enrique was having phone issues or something.

They were three hours into the surgery and Alexis needed a break from the waiting room. She grabbed her phone and let her sister and brother know that she was going out for some fresh air.

"Hey, I'm going to head downstairs for some fresh air. Do y'all want anything?"

"Nah, I'm good," Eric responded.

"Yes, bring me something from the vending machine and stop by Starbucks to get me an iced coffee."

"You always take things too far, Monica. I'm not a damn Uber Eats."

"Well, hell you asked if we wanted anything."

Monica and Eric both looked at each other and said, "A closed mouth don't get fed."

"Hush, I'm not bringing all that shit back. I'll get you something from the vending machine and a bottle of water."

"Thank you, baby girl."

Alexis rolled her eyes and exited the waiting room. She was headed downstairs when she heard a familiar voice call her name. She didn't turn around immediately because she knew she had to be tripping yet the voice was there again. She finally turned and there he was in the flesh. Staring at her with a big, boyish grin on his face.

"Enrique. What? How? When?"

"Hey, my brown skin girl. I wanted to come check on you."

"You left Spain early to come check on me? Umm, you shouldn't have."

"I should have and I did."

"Umm, I don't know what to say."

"Nothing, Don't say anything at all." Enrique closed the small distance between the two of them and brushed a light kiss across her lips. Alexis wanted more but she didn't want to be too inappropriate in the hospital. He pulled back slightly and kissed her forehead before pulling her back into a tight hug. "How are you?"

"A lot better since you're here."

"Were you headed out? How's your mom?"

"I was just coming out to get some fresh air. Mom is still in surgery." She hugged him tighter. "I can't believe you are here."

"Well, believe it. I'll be staying a few days if you are fine with it. I got a hotel in midtown."

"Umm, yes. That's fine. Thank you for coming to check on me."

"Of course."

Enrique wondered how he could tell her that from this point on she was his responsibility without sounding like a madman. He opted to not say anything at all. The last thing he wanted to do was push Alexis to make her feel rushed. Alexis and Enrique walked hand in hand, heading for the hospital's exit. They walked in silence for a little but Alexis finally broke the silence.

"What does this mean?"

"What does what mean?" he asked, looking at her for clarification.

"Altering your plans and flying all the way to Memphis to check on me."

"It means I care about you and wanted to make sure you were okay. To make sure you didn't need any additional support other than that of your family and friends."

"That's it?"

"Do you want it to mean more?"

"I just want to be clear about what it means."

"Do you need more clarification, Alexis?"

"No. Thank you so much."

"Of course. Now, come here and let me greet you properly."

Enrique pulled Alexis into his arms again and they shared a kiss. Not just any kiss but a kiss that he felt all in his groin. He knew she felt it too because she let out a slow moan. Not the one to pull back first, Enrique continued caressing her tongue with his. Alexis finally pulled back to breathe. She was panting and he enjoyed the look she wore on her face. A look of satisfaction and pleasure but also a look of wanting more. If it were up to him, she would get more and then some.

"Thanks for my proper greeting. We can walk to the end of this sidewalk and then we should probably head back. Monica's ass wants me to play Uber Eats and pick up all kinds of stuff."

"Works for me. If you're not ready for me to meet them, I can head back to my hotel and check on you a little later. I don't want any extra stress on you right now."

"Oh no, it's fine. They need to know you came all this way to check on me and our mom."

"Are you sure?"

"Yes, unless you don't want to meet them right now."

"I'm good either way. Your call."

"Cool. You get to meet my over-the-top sister, Monica, and my laidback brother, Eric."

"These descriptions."

Alexis winked and they headed back towards the hospital. Once they were inside, they found the vending machine and then they made their way to Starbucks. She and Enrique finally made it back to the waiting area. She was a tad bit nervous about the message it would send to them that he cut his trip early to travel to Memphis to check on her but she was excited that he would get to meet two of the most important people in her world, her sister and brother.

Alexis walked into the waiting room with Enrique following close behind her. It obviously had not registered with Monica that Enrique was with Alexis.

"About damn time, Lexie. I thought you had gotten lost." Eric was a much better observer than Monica. Mainly because he didn't spend his time finding something to fuss about like Monica. He stood to greet Enrique. It wasn't until he stood that Monica finally noticed him. Alexis was grinning as her sister stood there looking horrified.

"Umm, I didn't know you were bringing company back."

"I didn't either. Monica and Eric, this is Enrique. Enrique, meet my sister and brother."

Enrique and Eric shook hands. Monica stuck her hand out but Enrique pulled her in for a quick hug and a kiss on the cheek. If Alexis didn't know any better, she would say the heifer was blushing.

Monica looked at Alexis and said, "I see why you like him. He's charming."

Alexis just smiled as she felt obligated to give them an explanation. "Enrique surprised me by flying into Memphis to check on me and Mom."

"I'm here to support so if you guys need anything like food or something I can grab it for you."

Eric simply responded with a 'thanks man' but Monica was going to be Monica.

"So, you flew back from Spain to check on my baby sister?"

"Sure did."

Monica sat down with a smirk on her face. Alexis knew she would hear about it later. They all sat in silence for a while. Enrique and Eric started talking about whatever guys talk about. They settled into a comfortable conversation. Monica tapped Alexis on the shoulder to step into the hallway. Her ass couldn't wait any longer. Alexis rolled her eyes and they both got up and headed out.

"So, you didn't tell me things were this serious."

"What are you talking about? Nothing is serious."

"Alexis, come on. You can't possibly think it's not serious when he just flew halfway around the world to check on you."

"I don't know, Monica. I asked him what it meant and he said it didn't mean anything."

"Girl, please. No man is flying from Spain to Memphis to check on someone and provide emotional support when it's not serious."

"I can only go off what he tells me. I mean we've only known each other for a few weeks."

"Sometimes, it only takes one encounter. It's more than serious."

Alexis did that nervous thing she always does and started fiddling with her hair and then her hands. "You think so?"

"I know so and you know what else I know?"

"What?"

"You deserve it and so much more. Let's go and see if they have an update on Momma."

As Alexis and Monica entered the waiting area, the doctor called for the Carter family. They all rushed to get the update. Enrique stood slightly behind Alexis.

"Your mom did great in surgery. We performed a full hysterectomy. We will continue to monitor everything over the next few months but there's no reason she won't make a full recovery. She's in a great deal of pain right now and we will get her set up in her room shortly. Someone will let you know when she's in her room."

They all replied, "Thank you."

The doctor turned and exited. Alexis let out a sigh and Enrique placed his hand at the small of her back. She leaned into him.

"Do you need to go freshen up or get some real food? It could be a little while before she's in her room," he suggested.

"Yes, I want to get some food. Do you mind if I invite Eric and Monica?"

"Of course not."

"Hey. Do y'all want to go grab a bite to eat with Enrique and I?"

"Nah, we are good," Eric said.

"Wait, how are you speaking for me though?" Monica replied.

"Because you just had vending machine snacks and iced coffee. You're good."

"I guess I'm good because my new daddy said so."

Alexis laughed. One thing for sure, Monica did not like anyone telling her what to do. She knew her sister would let their brother have it once they left. She also knew Eric was giving her and Enrique some alone time and she appreciated him for that.

The next couple of days went by so quickly. Alexis and Enrique spent a lot of time together when she wasn't at the hospital with her mom. She would have to be in the hospital a few more days. Enrique had been a godsend. He catered to Alexis' every need. She definitely was starting to feel like their "relationship" was more than what either of them were saying. He made sure she ate timely, got rest, and didn't have to drive back and forth. He had become her personal chauffeur. She was sad that it was time for him to head back to Austin. She would miss his presence and the peace that came with it.

CHAPTER NINETEEN

Alexis had spent the last three weeks in Memphis and Mississippi. She was heading back to Atlanta but would be making frequent trips home to spend more time with her mom. Eric returned home shortly after their mom was released from the hospital. Of course, Monica lived in the area so it was great spending time with her.

Alexis still didn't know what was happening with her and Enrique but she was actually enjoying every moment of it. He was often the topic in her therapy sessions. It was now time for her to get all her work projects back on track and focus on her next business venture. Life was good and she was finally in a really good space, mentally and emotionally. It was hard to believe a little over a year ago she felt like she would never feel this good about her life. Thank goodness for time, therapy, and temporary circumstances and emotions.

While Alexis enjoyed her time with Monica and her mom, she was also very excited to get back in her own space. She hoped the creative juices would start to flow now that she was back home. She needed to get a lot of writing done. She decided she wouldn't nap on the short fifty-minute flight but she would start compiling her to do list and planning her schedule. It was about to be hectic for the next couple of months. Her being back in Atlanta would be the real test for her and Enrique. She just hoped that they could keep the same energy they've had since meeting in Madrid.

Wow, she thought to herself. She had to travel halfway around the world to find the most amazing guy. Life would definitely have it where they lived states away but at least he was stateside. She hoped they would be able to figure out how to make things work. She also knew she needed to take things one day at a time. Enrique just said it was nothing serious so she had to believe him until he said otherwise. His words were a little deceitful because his actions said it was more. But Alexis learned her lesson and would trust what he was saying. Although, deep down she wanted it to be more.

Enrique was coming to visit in a couple of weeks. She knew his love for history so they were making a day trip to Macon to check out the Harriet Tubman Museum. They would spend the rest of their time chilling and enjoying each other's company. She had spoken with Monica a few times and each time her sister managed to bring up the fact that they were making an effort to spend more time together. She always said the same thing, "It seems serious to me."

Alexis would roll her eyes and change the subject.

It was already Saturday and Alexis was excited. She was meeting with a new brand strategist to try to get things back on track. She had been on her unofficial hiatus long enough. She hoped Amina was half as great as her reviews. Honestly, she was anxious because the last person she really connected with on this project wasn't who she thought she was. Or maybe she didn't know who she thought she was. Either way, it was a disaster for her life.

Amina and Alexis met at a coffee shop in East Point. It was a nice, quaint coffee shop tucked off the beaten path. Alexis immediately liked the vibes she got from Amina. She was definitely on her shit. She had an outline from their phone conversation and they spent the two-hour meeting brainstorming and preparing for next steps. One of her suggestions was for Alexis to make her social media pages more relatable. She wanted her to post more of her personal life as opposed to only posting about business. Of course, Alexis was hesitant but she knew there was truth to what Amina said. Alexis promised to start posting more relatable content for her followers.

She would start with posting at least three times a week. She could go back and post pics from her most recent travels and anything upcoming that she had. It was helpful that Alexis liked taking random pics of things and people when she was out. She would also post some of her outfits since she considered herself to be a fashionista. She felt good after her meeting with Amina and they made plans to link up again in a couple of weeks. By then, Alexis would have posted some content and Amina would give her an evaluation.

The next week went by quickly. It was Thursday night and Enrique was due in town Friday afternoon. His flight arrived at 3:20.

Excitement took over Alexis as she arrived at the airport a lot earlier than expected. She sat in the cell phone parking lot awaiting Enrique's arrival. She decided to make her first "personal" post on her business social media. Honestly, she hadn't been on social media a lot since the debacle with Remington. Her last post on her business page was almost a year ago. She decided to post a few pics from her trip to Spain. She posted a pic of her in her fancy red dress, a pic of the oldest restaurant, and random pics from Baga, Ax-les Thermes, and Andorra. Her caption read: I'm back! I know it's been a while but life was happening. However, I wanted to share a few pics from my most recent travels: Madrid & Barcelona, Baga, Ax-les Thermes, and Andorra. Did y'all know Andorra was a country? I didn't but I appreciate my personal tour guide for the experience and all the knowledge shared. *heart*

For whatever reason, sharing that content had given her anxiety all week. But it wasn't too bad once she hit post. It shared to her Facebook and Instagram immediately. She needed to reset her Twitter password and she wasn't about to go through that right now. She patiently sat in her car waiting to get word from Enrique. After about a twenty-minute wait, she finally got a text.

Enrique: Hey brown skin girl! Just landed. Headed to the train and then baggage claim. I'll be at door S4 after I grab my bag. I'll text when I have my luggage.

Alexis: Yay! Great. Can't wait to see you.

Enrique: You have no idea.

Alexis sat in her car with the biggest grin on her face. He was really here. She couldn't wait to taste his lips on hers and lean into his masculine frame. She really did miss him. Lord, help her. Alexis' thoughts were interrupted by a text message and she thought it was Enrique, but it was Reign in their group text.

Reign: Has your new boyfriend made it yet?

Alexis: We are not boyfriend and girlfriend but yes he has. And I'm hella excited.

Brooklyn: Sure. Have fun and we are doing dinner on Tuesday to get all the details.

Reign: All of them. Leave nothing out.

Alexis: Whatever. Dinner sounds good. Reign are you cooking?

Reign: Hell no. I'll order takeout though.

Brooklyn: Go figure. The best cook in the group and she never cooks.

Alexis: Right. Okay, I'm pulling around to pick up Senor Manuel. Talk to y'all later. Love!

Brooklyn: Have fun. Get laid, too. Love.

Reign: Yes, get laid. Love.

Alexis pulled around to S4 and caught a glimpse of Enrique. He was so damn fine. If she had to say so herself, he complimented her well. She pulled up in front of him and let her window down.

"Hey. Need a ride?"

"Hey brown skin girl. Yes, I do if I'm riding with you."

He grabbed his luggage and headed to her trunk. Alexis popped the trunk and Enrique threw his bags in. Literally threw them in and hopped in her truck so quickly. He barely adjusted his seat before he was leaning over the console to capture her mouth with his. They both were lost in the kiss until an Atlanta police officer tapped on the window to move the car. He was yelling something about active loading and unloading only. They both looked at each other and laughed.

"Welcome to Atlanta where they are too serious about keeping these lines moving."

"Well, it is the busiest airport in the world."

"Do you want to grab something to eat?"

"No, I'm fine. I had an early lunch with Mom before I caught my flight."

"Okay. Well, to my house we go."

For some odd reason, Alexis had a ball of nerves roll through her. Anytime she got nervous, she would have sweat pop up on her nose and her mouth would get really dry. Her other indication was fiddling with her hair. All three were happening. Enrique obviously noticed.

"Are you nervous?"

"No, why do you say that?" Alexis tried to sound calm.

"One, you are not a good liar. Two, you like to fiddle with your hair when you are nervous or anxious."

"Wow. How do you know that?"

"I'm observant. I noticed in Spain and confirmed it when you were at the hospital during your mom's surgery."

"You really are observant."

"So, what has you so nervous?"

"Umm, I haven't had anyone at my new place but Brooklyn, Reign, and Justice."

"That's what has you nervous?"

"Kind of. Just thinking about what it means with you here staying at my house."

"It means whatever we decide it means. We can talk about it later if you want. But no pressure."

"I'd like that a lot."

Alexis blew out a deep breath. She needed to get her shit together because she wanted to have a relaxing weekend. The airport wasn't far from her house so after about fifteen minutes they were pulling into her neighborhood.

"I like that this neighborhood is gated. Are these new?"

"Yes, they are. The gated part is one of the things that sold me on the community."

"I didn't think you would be in a townhouse community though. Just figured you would want a yard and all that good stuff."

"I have a small space out back but I didn't want to be responsible for yard maintenance and all of that."

"Understood. Is this your forever home?"

"Not at all. It's my right now home."

"Oh good."

Alexis ignored that part because she didn't want to read too much into it. They pulled into her garage, Enrique grabbed his bags, and they went into the house.

"Let's get your bags put up and I'll give you a quick tour and show you where everything is. We can walk the neighborhood if you want as well. We have a swimming pool, tennis court, dog park, clubhouse but most importantly sidewalks for me to run."

"Sounds good to me."

It was obvious by his response that he was distracted. Alexis looked up to see what had grabbed his attention and he was staring at photos she had taken at her most recent photo shoot.

"I took those right before going on vacation. Photo shoots are part of my self-care. I just love doing them."

"You look absolutely gorgeous in these. How often do you do your photo shoots?"

"Umm, just whenever I feel it in my spirit. Sometimes, twice a year or more. But definitely at least twice a year."

"Nice. I want a copy of this picture."

He pointed to the picture where she was sitting in a rocking chair with a sparkly black dress on that showed off her long brown legs. Alexis giggled but Enrique wore an expression of seriousness.

"Oh, you are serious?"

"Absolutely."

He turned and headed up the stairs. Alexis followed closely behind him. She let him put his luggage in the primary bedroom and then quickly showed him around upstairs before they made their way downstairs. They spent the rest of the afternoon and evening talking and occasionally paying attention to what was on the television.

"We should order takeout because I'm not cooking tonight."

"But you are going to cook at some point?" Enrique asked with a raised brow.

"Yeah, I'll cook on Sunday."

"Oh cool. I must be special if you are cooking."

Alexis blushed. He was special. "Maybe. Oh yeah, we will leave here around nine o'clock to head out for our adventure tomorrow."

"I'll be ready. Now, come here. I want to feel you against me."

Alexis didn't put up any fight. She sat by Enrique and laid her head on his chest. He leaned in and kissed her forehead before placing a kiss on her collarbone. This was heaven for Alexis. He was so gentle and kind. She needed the kind more than anything.

"How is your mom?"

"She's a lot better. Thanks for asking."

"Of course."

They sat in silence for a while and it was the most peaceful Alexis had been in the past few weeks.

"I'm going to shower and get ready for bed. You're more than welcome to stay down here and watch television."

"Nah, I think I'll shower, too. I know tomorrow will be a long day."

Alexis and Enrique headed upstairs. Enrique grabbed his luggage and pulled out his toiletries and sleepwear. Alexis couldn't help but wonder how he usually sleeps at home. She wouldn't be surprised if he slept naked. What a sight that must be.

They both retreated to their respective bathrooms to prepare for bed. Alexis was looking forward to snuggling up against Enrique and being woken up by his kisses in the morning. She showered and did her nightly face care regime and moisturized her body. Just as she was exiting the bathroom, Enrique entered her room with sleep pajamas and shirtless. The shirtless part is what was doing it for her. She knew he had an amazing body but damn he was so fine. She didn't try to hide her wandering eyes and he didn't seem to mind being on display.

They both stood still and stared at each other. Alexis eventually broke eye contact but before she could say anything Enrique closed the distance between the two of them. He pulled her into him and began assaulting her mouth. He didn't hold anything back and she didn't mind. Time stood still as they explored each other's mouths. Enrique finally pulled back and the heat Alexis saw in his eyes told her everything she needed to know. He wanted her and she definitely wanted him. The response her body was giving told her that she more than wanted him. She needed him.

"You say the word and I'll stake claim," Enrique said.

"I want you," Alexis responded.

That was all the confirmation Enrique needed as he walked Alexis over to the bed. He first removed the ponytail holder she had placed in her hair. Her twists came tumbling down to her shoulders. He then motioned for her to lay on the bed and she obliged. Before Alexis knew what was happening she was lying on the bed in only her lace black panties.

Enrique rubbed his hands down both of Alexis' legs. "You are so beautiful and brown. I love your smooth skin and long legs." He leaned down and placed a kiss on her hip. While he kissed her thigh, his hands caressed her arms. Eventually, he made his way to her stomach and began placing soft kisses around her navel.

"Umm, thank you."

Alexis was a little shy at the assessment Enrique was making while she lay mostly naked. Instinctively, she wanted to cover her body, but she didn't have any way to do so. She squirmed under his watchful eye. It was a little unsettling yet his mouth felt great on her body.

He continued to study her body and place small kisses all over her. He began at her forehead and trailed kisses down the left side of her body. He did the same thing on the right side before eventually making his way back to her stomach. He traced circles around her navel with his tongue. A small moan escaped Alexis' lips. It had been so long since she experienced a man's touch. Well, more than a year but too damn long for her liking.

Enrique continued tracing circles around her navel while he massaged her breasts. Alexis didn't know how much more she could take but she was getting close to the edge. Her moans were soft and low but with each flick of his tongue they became louder. Enrique brought his mouth up to her breast and began licking and sucking her right nipple while expertly rolling her left nipple. The sensations were overwhelming.

He finally pulled back and reached down to remove her now drenched panties. In any other situation, Alexis would be ashamed but she wanted him to know just how turned on he made her. He didn't seem to mind anyway. He placed one finger inside of her and Alexis let out an unexpected yelp. He then placed another finger inside and expertly started moving his fingers. He captured her mouth with his and swallowed any additional sounds she thought about making. It seemed like an eternity had gone by before Enrique replaced his fingers with his mouth.

Alexis exploded instantly. She had been on edge for so long and now she finally got the long overdue orgasm. She could feel the smile on his lips as he continued massaging her clit with his tongue. Alexis wanted more. She wanted him. Hell, honestly she needed him.

"Umm, baby I want to feel you."

Enrique pulled back and his eyes darken by at least two shades. He didn't say anything as he got up from the bed and went over to his toiletry bag and removed a box of condoms. Placing it on the nightstand after taking one from the box. He then removed his pajama bottoms and boxers. Alexis stared in amazement but she was nervous as hell, too. She began to fidget with her hair.

"Relax. We will go as slow as you need to go."

"Okay."

That was the only response she managed. Enrique tore open the foil wrapper and threw the empty pack on the nightstand. He covered himself with the condom before positioning himself over Alexis.

"Look at me. I want to remember the look on your face the moment I staked my claim."

Alexis opened her eyes and stared into his as he entered her. She winced at the pain but she knew it was temporary. Enrique continued to ease into her until she felt full. He stilled himself for a few moments, giving her time to adjust. He slowly began moving. It was a slow rhythm which Alexis appreciated at first. Due to it being such a long time since she last had sex and his size, she needed time to adjust. After a few minutes at a slow pace, she needed more. More force. More speed. More of him.

She thrusted her hips up to him and that was his cue. Enrique's thrusts became harder and faster. Alexis' body was soon on the brink of another orgasm.

"Open your eyes. I want you looking at me when you come for me." Alexis squeezed her eyes tighter because the sensations were so great. But then it all stopped. Enrique wasn't moving. The pleasure had subsided. She opened her eyes. "Keep your eyes open when you come for me, brown skin girl."

He slowly began moving again. His thrusts became harder and faster again. Alexis was right back where she was a few minutes ago. She looked away and noticed his pace slowed. She turned her head to look back at him and he increased his pace. *Oh, he's serious. He really wants me looking at him.* Her muscles tightened around him and she felt the onslaught of her orgasm coming fast. She screamed out his name as her release hit her hard.

Enrique followed behind her with his own release. He was careful not to collapse on top of her as he knew he would be too heavy. He rolled over to the side and got off the bed. He discarded the condom and then Alexis heard water running. She was so exhausted and quite honestly didn't want to interrupt her state of euphoria.

He came back into the room with a warm towel and wiped Alexis before returning the towel back to the bathroom. He then got back in bed and pulled Alexis into his side. He placed light kisses on her collarbone, earlobe, and neck.

"Alexis Carter, you are mine."

"Is that so? One night of sex and I'm yours, huh?"

"Absolutely. You were mine before now but you're definitely mine now."

"I didn't realize it worked like that."

"It does. Now, get some rest, my brown skin girl."

"Didn't know you were so demanding, Senor Manuel."

"You will learn my ways soon enough. Sleep."

He placed a kiss on the back of her neck. Alexis snuggled in closer to him and felt sleep fast approaching. Enrique, on the other hand, wasn't interested in sleeping. He had too many things to figure out. He lay with his chin in the top of Alexis' hair, wearing the biggest grin on his face. She was his and had no idea what that meant for her.

The next morning Alexis woke up to find Enrique had already gotten out of the bed. Disappointment rushed through her. She wanted to be greeted by his forehead kiss and her new favorite collarbone kiss. Wishful thinking. She pulled herself out of bed and noticed how sore she was. An instant smile touched her lips. She hopped in the shower, brushed her teeth, and threw on her satin robe. She intentionally didn't put on anything under the robe. They could skip the museum and spend all their time in the house having sex if it were up to her. She made her way downstairs to find

Enrique sitting at the kitchen island with his laptop open.

"Good morning, Senor."

"Good morning my brown skin, sexy as sin Alexis."

She giggled. "Really, all of that. Did you sleep well?"

"Not really."

"I'm sorry is the bed not comfortable because we can try sleeping in the guest room tonight."

"Nope, just wasn't sleepy. Had a lot to process and think through."

"Oh. You want to talk about it?"

"Actually, I do but I know we need to get the day started so we can discuss later."

"Umm, okay. Is everything okay though? Is it about last night?" The nervousness was all in Alexis' voice.

"It's absolutely about last night but it's not what you think. You worry too much."

"I just don't like suspense."

"Fine. I was up all night trying to figure out how we are going to make this work. Because like I said last night you are mine now. So, I have to figure this out. Happy?"

"You keep saying I'm yours like I'm property. It sounds very domineering."

"You are not property, but last night was a game changer and I'm staking claim, Alexis."

"What does that mean? Are you saying you want to be in a relationship?"

"Yes. Do you?"

"Umm, if we can figure out how to make it work, but honestly I'm nervous."

"Why?"

"I don't know because my last relationship was local and it still didn't work out."

"Look," Enrique sighed. "I'm not your ex. Quite frankly, he was an idiot. It will work. Now, let's get dressed or either eat breakfast so we can start our day."

Alexis was a little taken aback by his tone. Not that it was mean but it was so matter of fact. She couldn't say that she didn't like it but she couldn't say it was something she had grown accustomed to.

"Fine, I'll make breakfast and then we can leave shortly after," she whispered. Enrique's eyes softened.

"Come here. I didn't mean to sound harsh. Thank you for making breakfast." Enrique placed a light kiss on her collarbone. Alexis' body defied her and melted into his. He rubbed her breast through her robe and was pleased to know she wasn't wearing a bra. "Do you have on anything under this robe?"

"No. Is that a problem?"

"Absolutely not."

He grabbed her hands and walked into the living room and motioned for her to lay down. And she did. He opened her robe before kneeling in front of her. He pulled and tugged at both nipples then pinched them hard before pulling and tugging again. He then dropped his hands and pulled Alexis to the edge of the couch and slowly began licking her thighs and eventually making his way to her vagina. She moaned and with each moan he increased his intensity. His tongue entered her and Alexis lost it. She screamed his name. He kept right on until she released in his mouth. She heard him slurping and then she felt his mouth on her now sensitive clit. He sucked slightly but the pressure kept building. Before long, he was applying a lot of pressure. She was close to another orgasm and he knew it. He put two fingers inside her and began to move them in a back and forth motion. Alexis came again. This time Enrique removed his mouth from her clit and removed his fingers. He licked her juices off his fingers and then pulled her up off the couch.

"You still want to make breakfast or do you want to stop somewhere?"

"Let's just stop somewhere."

"Okay, I'll head upstairs to get dressed."

"I'll be up soon."

"Don't overthink this. Us."

Alexis bit her lip as a little anxiety began to creep back into her state of euphoria. "I'll try not to."

Chapter Twenty

So much had happened since Enrique's visit to Atlanta. Alexis and Enrique had a blast at the museum and the entire weekend was amazing. She was blown away by all the sex they had but she definitely appreciated it.

She, Brooklyn, and Reign got together for their dinner as promised and she gave them a high-level overview of the weekend. Brooke seemed to believe that Enrique was into dominatrix but Reign didn't think so. Alexis just knew he was serious about letting her know she was his. He said it often and showed it with his actions. Something definitely clicked in him. He was still her sweet, handsome, fun, adventurous senor but he was also very protective. More than what he was before.

It was official, they were a couple. They agreed that they would meet up at least twice a month. True to their word, Alexis was headed to Austin to hang out with him. She was nervous because she would be staying at his home and she would also meet his mom. The latter was more nerve wracking than anything.

Alexis was excited that she had revitalized her social media pages thanks to Amina.

Their meeting last week went great and she was excited about everything she planned for her brand. One thing that kept nagging her though was the obsession one of her followers had with her. It wasn't a name she was familiar with but this person commented on every pic and liked every post. Amina said she should only be worried if the person starts to inbox her which they hadn't but Alexis got an eerie feeling anytime her notification dinged and it was from him. Hell, it could be a *her* for all she knew. Her gut said something was off but she tried not to worry about it. She didn't bring it up to Enrique because he was already overprotective.

He did follow her on social media so if he noticed anything he hadn't mentioned it. It just seemed weird that this person only posted pics of other people traveling. Alexis had combed through the timeline and couldn't identify anything personal about the owner of the account. She shook off the thoughts.

Today, Alexis made a post of her outfit. She was wearing a cute crop top shirt that said: **empowered**. She also had a cute crossbody, leggings, and animal print shoes that matched. The caption on the post read: What makes you feel empowered? For me, it's being loved properly, traveling, and helping others. Chime in.

It was a simple post and a fairly simple question. Alexis awaited her flight departure. She instantly got a ding from her IG page and it was the creepy follower. Of course, they liked the photo and responded to her question. *I feel empowered when I love properly, travel, and help others.* Alexis rolled her eyes. See, it was this creepy shit that made her want to delete this person. She didn't bother with a response.

Alexis finally arrived in Austin and Enrique was curbside to pick her up. He hopped out of his SUV and greeted her with a kiss. And it felt amazing. Damn, she missed him. The electric charge she felt never disappointed when he looked at her and their lips touched. She noticed that he held her a little longer than usual. Not that she was complaining. It felt great to be back in his arms. She let her body meld into his and relaxed a little more. *This was heaven on earth.*

"Hey baby! Welcome to Austin. Let me grab your bags."

"Hey, Señor Manuel. Gracias."

Alexis handed him the bags and Enrique opened the door for her before putting them in the trunk and making his way back to the driver's side. Alexis noticed how less busy this airport was compared to Atlanta. In Atlanta, the police would have come by knocking on the window by now, yelling for you to move your car.

"How was your flight?"

"It was fine. What's the plan for the day?"

"I figured we would chill for a little and then have dinner with my mom later." Alexis didn't say anything but she started fiddling with her hair. "Alexis, you have nothing to worry about. My mom is very laid back and she will love you."

"That's easy for you to say, it's your mom."

"You will see for yourself. Nothing to worry about. Anyway, tomorrow we will go to Six Flags."

"Oh yay! Wait, I don't like rides."

"It'll be fun. Trust me." Alexis rolled her eyes and relaxed in her seat. She had to get through dinner tonight. "Alexis, don't overthink this. Do you want to stop and grab something to eat or go straight home?"

It was something about the way Enrique put emphasis on going straight home that made her smile, inwardly.

"Let's just go to your house. I'm sure you have something for me to snack on. Plus, I'm not really hungry."

"Home, it is. I did buy a few of your favorites so you will be good."

"Huh?" She smiled at his thoughtfulness. "Like what?"

"Apples, almond butter, pineapple juice, even got some disgusting ass beet juice, fresh pineapples, a bag of cuties, and kettle corn."

"Oh, so you think you know me?"

"Nah, but I'm observant. I know you love snacking though."

"Thank you. And thank you for making them healthy snacks."

Alexis leaned over and kissed his cheek. The boyish grin that spread across his face was all the assurance she needed. She knew he would make sure she was straight at all times. Alexis relaxed and closed her eyes.

"Are you tired?"

"No, just relaxing. Ready to chill for the day."

At that moment, Alexis' phone dinged. It was an alert from her IG account. The creepy follower sent her a DM.

[@1284love]: Are you traveling?

Alexis stared at the screen contemplating if she should respond or not. Enrique must have noticed the change in her body language. She had suddenly become very tense and she was positive she wore the expression on her face as well.

"Is everything okay?"

"Umm, yes."

"Are you sure? Is your mom okay?"

"Yes, it's just that I have a creepy follower on IG."

"Creepy how?"

"They like everything I post and occasionally make little weird comments. Amina says it's nothing for me to worry about but my gut tells me something is off."

"Always trust your gut, baby. What do you need me to do?"

"Nothing. Absolutely nothing. You are kind of overprotective."

"As I should be and it can definitely intensify if need be."

Alexis rolled her eyes and laid her phone in her lap. She was just going to block this person. She was really inclined to believe it was a guy, too. No female had time to be stalking another female because of a few travel pics and outfits of the day. Yeah, definitely a dude. He probably was a loner.

They finally pulled into the parking garage for Enrique's downtown condo. She shouldn't have been surprised by the modern, luxury look of the building. It was eight stories high. He had never mentioned what floor he lived on and she never thought to ask but she was positive he would be on the top floor. They drove to the top of the parking garage that required special access. Enrique had to tap his parking pass before pulling into a reserved parking spot with his name on it. She also noticed that there were only five other parking spots. Alexis hopped out and quickly took note that all the parking spots had his name on it.

"Does this whole top floor of the parking garage belong to you?"

"Maybe. Is that a bad thing?"

"No, I'm just asking."

"Well, yes, it does."

"Wow. I can only imagine what this condo will look like inside."

Enrique smiled but didn't respond. His only hope was that she liked it enough to call it home one day. His mom made sure it was nicely decorated and he was sure Alexis would appreciate that. He was positive that she would after seeing her place in Atlanta. He grabbed her bags and they walked over to the elevator. Enrique pressed his thumb to have his fingerprint read and the glass elevator doors opened. Alexis was in awe. Not just because of the luxury condo but of him. He was so lowkey and was living like a damn king in Austin.

Of course, he was living like a king. She giggled to herself. They went up one floor and stepped off the elevator. Again, Enrique pressed his thumb into the keypad and the door opened to his condo. Alexis was immediately drawn to all the natural light and the view of downtown Austin. She didn't really pay attention to much else as she sauntered over to the windows to enjoy the view more.

"It's one of the reasons I decided on this location. The view is probably the best in the city."

"It's absolutely gorgeous. Do you sit on your balcony much?"

"All the time. When I can stand the Texas heat."

"Hmmm, we could have some fun out here."

Alexis looked up to see the heat in Enrique's eyes as he left her luggage by the front entrance and made his way over to her. She grinned and anticipated what was about to happen. When Enrique reached her, he pulled her into his arms and assaulted her mouth with his tongue. Alexis could barely keep up with his rhythm. She finally pulled back to get her bearings but Enrique kept his intense gaze on her.

"We could definitely have a lot of fun out there and maybe we will. For now, I would love to get you relaxed until later. A lot is to come later."

"That sounds promising and exciting."

Alexis needed a moment to gather herself after the kiss. She didn't even request a tour because being in close proximity with him was doing a number on her senses and her desire for sex. While she enjoyed sex with him, she wanted to do more than moan his name all weekend.

"Will you show me the restroom?"

"Of course, you can use the one in the primary bedroom. I can give you a tour."

"Maybe later. I need to freshen up really quick."

"Okay. Down the hall to your left is the primary bedroom."

Alexis headed in that direction. She noticed Enrique stood still and watched her walk away. She was nervous. She needed to get her shit together. Damn, she meant to grab her phone so she could send her customary 'made it' text messages. After a couple minutes of breathing and gathering herself, Alexis exited the restroom.

Enrique had placed her luggage in a corner in his bedroom. She headed down the hall to find him standing in the kitchen. It was then that she paid attention to his home. She had been captivated by the view but the décor and furniture were amazing as well. She loved the open concept but each area had a defined space. His kitchen was a cook's dream come true. The kitchen island could easily fit eight. There was plenty of cabinet space and prep space. She couldn't fathom why he needed a double oven but there it was.

His living room was accompanied by a tan leather sectional and cream-colored accent chairs. His decor included accents of gold and bronze. The pieces were nicely put together so it wasn't too masculine. Of course, his television was massive. It had to be eighty inches or more.

"Okay, I'm ready for the tour now."

Enrique stood and walked toward Alexis. "Well, as you can see this is the living room, dining room, and kitchen."

"I love the open concept. It's very nice. Who helped decorate?"

"My mom, of course. I would've had it all dark with browns, blacks, and grays."

"Of course, you would have. These paintings. Are they local artists?"

"Some of them are but a majority are from Spain. Both my parents love art so my dad sends me paintings every so often."

"They are gorgeous."

Alexis was captivated by one particular abstract painting. It was very similar to some of the ones she had seen in the restaurant while in Madrid. They included metallics but most of these were gold and bronze to keep in line with his decor and color scheme.

"Thank you."

They continued down the hall and bypassed his room as she had already seen that. He then showed her three other guest bedrooms. "Let me show you my office."

Alexis was puzzled because they had seen every bit of the condo. Enrique walked her to a door that led to a set of stairs. They descended and Alexis was blown away. It wasn't just an office. It was a masterpiece. He had a built-in bookcase on one wall. The other wall had lots of natural light from the floor to ceiling windows and the other wall was filled with accolades, awards, and lots of other cool stuff like more paintings. He had a smaller wall with framed blueprints. Alexis walked over to that particular wall. The first thing she noticed was the blueprint for Serenity Luxury Condos. He did the blueprint for this building.

"This is your building?"

"I'm part owner, yes."

"Who owns the other part?"

"My dad and my uncle."

"So, it makes sense now. You're the owner so of course you will have all the amenities and more. Smart, senor."

"Glad you approve, senorita."

Alexis looked over at Enrqiue's desk which was way more organized than she ever kept hers. "This place has a lot of natural light. I love the vibe here."

"Nah, baby we are the vibe. Every place feels like this when I'm with you."

She wanted him. In his office. On his desk. And she would have him. As she walked towards his desk, Enrique picked up on the plan and was in action before Alexis could make her intentions clear. It was in her body language. Her hips swayed more and her walk became more seductive. She licked her lips as she made her way to him. She felt the heat at the junction of her thighs and in that very moment her breasts became heavier. She was definitely ready for him.

CHAPTER TWENTY-ONE

Alexis kicked off her shoes. Before she could reach to remove her shirt, Enrique was there to assist. He pulled her shirt over her head as he stood behind her placing light kisses at the spine of her neck. He unclasped her bra and let her breasts fall free. He let the bra fall to the floor and took both hands to cup her breasts, pulling and pinching her nipples. Alexis let out a low gasp and his penis stood at attention. Enrique turned her to face him and then pulled at the waist of her leggings. She began to slowly remove them.

He stared as Alexis stood there in front of him with nothing but her animal print boy short panties on. The heat in his eyes intensified as they roamed her body. It took a lot of restraint for him not to become very primal with her. He could stare at her body all day but he could also do other stuff to her body that would bring them both pleasure.

Enrique leaned in and took Alexis' right breast into his mouth. She let out a soft moan. He continued the back and forth between both breasts. The primal groan that escaped his mouth told him he only had seconds before he lost it. He moved quickly behind his desk, opened his top right drawer, and pulled out a box of condoms.

Alexis met him with a questioning look.

"I knew we would end up down here at some point during the weekend." He smirked.

"Always so sure of yourself, Senor Manuel."

Enrique made quick work of his hands to undress himself. After he was fully undressed, he ushered Alexis to the desk and guided her on top. He didn't waste any time once she was laying on her back. He removed the animal print panties and the smell of her womanhood enveloped his nostrils. He needed her in his mouth now. His mouth covered her and he knew he was in heaven with Alexis. She must have been excited because it didn't take long for her to come in his mouth.

He stood, tore open the foil packet, and rolled the condom down the length of him. Pulling Alexis to the edge of the desk, he entered her slowly. The feel of her surrounding him was almost more than he could handle. His strokes were long and slow. It wasn't long before Alexis was begging for more intensity and he gave her just what she wanted.

They spent hours in his office space christening every surface suitable for their activities. Enrique knew Alexis needed her rest and as much as he wanted to wake her from her much needed nap, he didn't. He figured she had finally recovered from the fun in the office space when he heard her in the room getting ready for dinner with his mom. He wished she wasn't so nervous about meeting his mom but he knew sex definitely had a way of relaxing her. He could say that was part of his plan all along but honestly, she was irresistible to him and it was hard to contain himself.

He knew Alexis expected them to dine at some fancy restaurant that required a dress code but he had assured her that his mom was laid back. He knew it was hard for her to believe until they pulled into a parking lot of a Mexican restaurant. That was one thing his mom and Alexis definitely had in common. They both loved tacos. He told Alexis they were going to one of his mom's favorite restaurants.

They parked and walked inside. Enrique spotted his mom immediately and they headed to the corner table where she sat.

"She is gorgeous," Alexis whispered.

"So are you, Alexis."

"Hey, Mom," Enrique greeted her with a kiss on the cheek.

"Hey, baby," she said, returning the kiss.

"Mom, this is Alexis. Alexis, this is my mom, Rose."

"Hi, Ms. Rose. Nice to meet you," Alexis responded and stuck out her hand.

"Girl, give me a hug. Nice to meet you." Alexis obliged and gave her a hug. "You are just as pretty as Enrique said you were."

"Awe, thank you. You are just as pretty as he said you were."

"Oh really?" She giggled.

They all sat down with Alexis sitting in the inside closest to the wall opposite of Enrique's mom. Enrique wore the biggest grin on his face. The two most important women in his world were in one place. It was a peace he couldn't explain but one he planned to relish in while the moment lasted. The waitress came and took their drink orders and shortly after, their food orders. It was the usual conversation for the three of them. Enrique was right. His mom was really laid back. By mid-dinner, Alexis had totally relaxed and enjoyed the company.

After dinner was over, they were saying their goodbyes when Ms. Rose pulled Alexis into a hug.

"I understand why he's so crazy about you," she whispered. "You are a true gem."

"Thank you," was all Alexis managed to whisper back.

"I hope I get to see the two of you before you head back to Atlanta, Alexis."

"Maybe tomorrow after Six Flags, Mom."

"Okay, I'll hold you to that son." Ms. Rose kissed Enrique on the cheek and everyone parted ways. When they got to the car Enrique looked over at Alexis.

"See, it wasn't that bad."

"Nah, it wasn't bad at all. Your mom really is laid back."

"I told you. She is very down to earth. Her presence is peaceful."

Alexis didn't say anything but he was right. His mom had a very calming presence much like her own mom. They rode home in silence. This time Enrique didn't take the elevator to get to his condo. They took a side door that again required a fingerprint entrance. This particular door led directly into the office space. The room still had the smell of their sex from earlier. It did something to Enrique's senses.

His body responded to the scents that they had left behind. He was slowly learning Alexis enough to know when she was ready and he could tell by the sway in her hips and her labored breathing. It was crazy how much he wanted her. In all honesty, he needed her. She was his calm and peace and she had no idea. Enrique continued walking to head upstairs. There was no doubt in his mind that she knew what he was doing. They made their way to the main living area and it was a matter of minutes before they both were out of their clothes and headed to his balcony.

He waited such a long time to experience this type of fun on his balcony but he knew it wouldn't be with just anyone. He now understood why the universe made him wait. The experience was like nothing he had ever felt. Sex with Alexis was mind blowing by itself but sex while admiring the Austin skyline in between orgasms was beyond anything he could fathom.

The next morning, he and Alexis headed to Six Flags for some adventure. As he expected, Six Flags was amazing. The rides weren't bad and he was surprised at how many Alexis actually rode. She was more adventurous than he thought. After Six Flags, they had dinner with his mom again but Enrique decided to order takeout and they chilled at his place. He figured the environment would be more relaxing for Alexis.

Enrique couldn't believe it was already time for Alexis to head back to Atlanta. He was already making plans for the next two weeks when they met up. He could tell Alexis was sad that time had gone by so fast. She seemed very melancholy all morning. She had less pep in her step. She must be feeling the same thing he was feeling. It was becoming increasingly difficult to leave and not see her for two whole weeks. They agreed to meet up in Memphis. Alexis would get there a few days early so she could spend time with her mom in Mississippi and Enrique would fly in later.

CHAPTER TWENTY-TWO

Alexis had plenty of content to post on her social media from her trip to Austin. She just didn't know what she wanted to post without sharing too much of her personal business. She loved the bubble she and Enrique lived in. No outside noise. Just the two of them enjoying each other's company. She decided to post a picture of her at Six Flags getting ready to ride the Goliath and the caption read: Let's see how this goes. I'm not the thrill-seeking type but I can be influenced every once in a while.

Her notifications dinged and she feared it was her creepy follower that she should probably block but to her surprise it was Enrique. He commented with two hearts. Alexis' face split into a grin. *Oh, so now we are commenting on each other's posts? This is about to get interesting.* Shortly after Enrique's comment, Alexis got a notification that the creepy follower liked her post but they didn't comment. She also noticed that they liked Enrique's comment. Weird. Maybe it is a female. Guys don't typically like other guy's comments unless it's sports related. It goes against their man code.

It was the Friday after Alexis left Austin. She, Brooklyn, Reign, and Justice were going out for dinner and drinks. Heavy emphasis on the drinks. Alexis left a little early so she and Reign could pre-game before meeting up with the other two. They sat around for an hour or so and caught up on everything that was happening with their relationships. Reign was giving an ex from college another chance. Things seemed to be going well so far and Alexis was happy for her.

It was apparent that Alexis was over the moon about Enrique. Crazy thing is she was excited about Remington but never this excited. She wanted to scream from the rooftop and tell the world how much she liked him. If she was being honest with herself, she was very much in love with Enrique. He hadn't said it but she felt loved by him as well. As if on cue, she received a text from him.

Enrique: Hey, my brown skin girl. Have fun tonight and let me know when you get in, no matter the time.

Alexis: Hey baby. Okay, I will. If you are awake, I'll give you a call when I'm on my way home.

Enrique: Okay. Be safe. *heart emoji*

"I'm assuming that's your lover boy because honey, you are smiling too damn hard for it to be anyone else," Reign chimed in.

"Hush but yeah he was just checking in with me."

"Y'all cute and shit. Aaron does the same thing."

"But you giving me a hard time," Alexis teased.

"Hell yeah, because I don't be grinning like a damn Cheshire cat."

"Whatever. He makes me smile."

"I know and I love it. I love him for that because you deserve to smile after that damn lifetime movie you lived through."

"Tell me about it. It just feels good and different. No funny moves being made. I feel like a priority."

"As you should. Now, let's take a shot," Reign said as she moved around her kitchen. "I don't want to hear shit about you don't take shots anymore."

"Damn. Fine. Just no patron for me. Those days are long gone. You have Don Julio?"

"Girl, of course, but yo' ass gone be messed up before long. Watch." Reign put two shot glasses on the counter before pulling a bottle from her collection. She filled them both before sliding one to Alexis.

"I'm only doing one shot tonight," Alexis said as she held the shot glass up.

Reign and Alexis toasted with their shot of Don Julio and headed out the door. They decided to carpool since Alexis had to pass back by Reign's to get home. They were blasting the latest Beyonce album and singing loud as hell. Reign drove fast as hell for no reason. Alexis knew they made it to Buckhead in record time from the south side. They entered the restaurant to find Justice seated by the front entrance. They were just waiting on Brooklyn. Shortly afterwards, Brooklyn arrived looking frazzled.

"Hey y'all. Sorry, I'm running a little late."

"No worries. We haven't been here too long," Reign said.

"Right, I'm just happy to be out of the house," Justice giggled.

"Let's get this night of fun started!" Alexis said.

They were quickly seated. The restaurant was busy but everything moved fairly quickly. The waitress took their drink and appetizer orders.

"So, Alexis, tell us about your Austin trip. How are things with you and the new boo?" Justice asked.

Alexis gave them a brief rundown of the trip to Austin. They were in awe of his condo and the fact that he co-owned the building. She spared her girl the details of the sexcapades but she mentioned that lots of sex was had. And it was. She told them about his mom and how cool she was. Clearly, Enrique gets his laid-back personality from her. The waitress returned to take their dinner orders just as Alexis was wrapping up her Austin story.

"Enrique and I will meet in Memphis next weekend. Then he wants to come back to Atlanta. I'll make sure y'all get to meet him then."

"Yes, honey. I need to meet this man. He has you glowing," Justice said.

"Exactly. Glowing and missing in action," Brooklyn responded.

"I just love it. Whatever he is doing I hope he keeps it up. Sis, you look happy," Reign spoke softly.

"Thank you," Alexis said. "I am."

"Good, now let's figure out what we gone do about my lil' single, lonely ass," Brooklyn laughed.

"Girl, you ain't hardly looking for a damn man," Alexis responded.

"Not right now but give me about three or four months."

"What's changing then?" Justice asked.

"Not a damn thang," Reigned answered.

They all burst into laughter. The rest of the night went smoothly. They finished dinner and decided to hit a lounge for drinks. Alexis had too much to drink. Her one shot minimum went out the window when Justice requested everyone take a shot. Who could turn down momma Justice? No one. Another shot of Don Julio coupled with four amaretto sours and Alexis had exceeded her quota for the month. She decided it would be best for her to just stay at Reign's for the night.

She texted Enrique to let him know.

Alexis: Hey baby. I had too much to drink. I'm going to crash at Reign's tonight.

Enrique: Are you okay?

Alexis: Yes, just don't think it's best for me to drive.

Enrique: Good. Call me in the morning.

Alexis: Okay, good night.

Enrique: Good night my brown skin girl.

Alexis and Reign made it back to Reign's house a little before 2 AM. Brooklyn and Justice had already text and said they made it home. All four of them were safe so Alexis made her way upstairs to the guest bedroom. She was tired and needed to get in the bed.

"Going to bed. I'm dog tired."

"Shit, I'm right behind you, Lexie. I haven't been out this long in a while."

"I know right."

"I'm going to call Aaron though so I won't go right to sleep."

"Ain't y'all cute."

"Take your drunk ass to bed. Good night."

"Good night, Reign."

Alexis made it home mid-morning on Saturday. She rushed in and showered before relaxing and calling Enrique. He didn't answer. Before she could put her phone down, she received a call that someone was at the gate needing to be buzzed in. She answered and was told it was a delivery for her so she accepted. She went to the door and was greeted with a bouquet of sunflowers. A huge grin came across her face. She immediately texted Enrique.

Alexis: Thanks for the flowers baby, I love them.

Alexis was very close to saying 'I love you, too' but she didn't. Fifteen minutes or so passed before Enrique called. Alexis answered on the first ring.

"Baby, thank you for the flowers."

"Umm, I didn't send you any flowers."

Alexis' smile faltered. "Stop playing."

"No, I'm not Alexis. I didn't send any flowers."

"Well, who sent them?"

"That's a good question."

"I just assumed they were from you and didn't bother looking for a card or anything."

Enrique didn't respond as Alexis made her way back to the kitchen to get a better look at the flowers. It was then that she noticed the lone, black rose in the midst of the sunflowers. Her body tensed.

"Alexis, are you there? Does it have a card?" She didn't need a card at this point to know who it was from. "Alexis, are you okay?"

"Umm, yes. I need to call you right back."

She didn't give Enrique time to respond because she needed to get her bearings. Why did he seek to find her? Why would he send flowers to her house? He shouldn't even have her address. It had been over a year and he decides to pop up fucking with her. Alexis took the vase of flowers and threw them in the big trash can outside. When she walked back into the house her phone was ringing. She knew it was Enrique. She needed to explain to him.

"Hello?" Alexis answered.

"Hey, what's going on? Are you okay?"

"Not really." Alexis' voice was a lot shakier than she wanted it to be.

"What the hell? Tell me what's going on or I'm catching the next flight out."

"That's not necessary. I received a bouquet of sunflowers and I thought they were from you. So, when you said they weren't I went looking for a card but then I saw it had a single black rose in the center of the sunflowers. Only one person I know sends black roses and that's my ex."

"Your ex, Remington? The asshole?"

"Yes, one and the same."

"Why the fuck would he be sending you flowers? Why does he have your address?"

"I don't know the answer to either one of them. My address is public record like all addresses are."

"I'll find out why though. I'm catching a flight out later today. I need to have a conversation with his hoe ass."

Alexis' body tensed even more. Enrique's tone and his language made her even more uncomfortable. She tried to take a few deep breaths but that only made her breathing more labored and shallower. She was counting to ten in her head to calm her nerves.

"Enrique, it's not that serious. I don't want to give him that kind of energy."

"I do. I want to give him the same energy he's trying to give you. You are clearly upset and you expect me to do nothing about it?"

"It's not a big deal. Really."

"It's a big deal. You are mine and I protect what's mine."

"Will you please calm down? This isn't helping me."

"Fine. What would you like me to do?"

"Calm down. And just don't give it too much thought. If it happens again, we can explore your route."

"So, I'm supposed to sit around and wait for him to send you more flowers?"

"My goodness. I hate this is happening."

"Me too. This is why I need to be closer. His punk ass would not try this if he knew you had someone in the same city as you."

Alexis didn't say anything. She could feel the anger in Enrique's voice. There had never been a time when she remembered him cursing like this. He was pissed. She was pissed as well. Her new home was her sanctuary and she didn't appreciate Remington sending his bad energy her way. She definitely would be burning some sage.

"Alexis, I will be making a trip to Atlanta sooner than expected."

"Baby, listen to me. You have to trust me. You don't have to. There's nothing to worry about. Remington just wants a response from me and when I don't give him one he will go back to his life."

"Nah, this ain't sitting well with me. What's your schedule this week?"

"I will see you on Friday. Remember? I leave for Mississippi on Wednesday afternoon."

"Remind me again, are you driving or flying?"

"I'm driving this time."

"I'll fly in on Wednesday morning and drive down with you."

"No, you will not. You already told me you have an important meeting on Thursday. This is not a big deal."

"It's not to you but to me it is. I'll take your word this time but this is the only time."

Alexis let out a deep sigh before changing the subject. She could tell Enrique was not happy but there really wasn't much that he could do and flying in from Austin seemed a little over-the-top. The conversation was off. The next few days were the same. The vibe and energy were off. Alexis was thrilled that it was finally Wednesday and she would be driving home to spend time with her mom and sister. She hadn't told either of them about Remington and the flowers.

CHAPTER TWENTY-THREE

It was finally time for Alexis to hit the road. She took a picture of her traveling outfit which happened to be a shirt that read: **Home is where the heart is.** The words were written through the shape of the state of Mississippi and were black with white lettering. She wore red leggings with black and white Michael Kors shoes and a black and white MK crossbody purse. She also wore her favorite red lipstick. The caption on her post read: Going to the place that always makes my heart smile. What's the one place you always feel safe? For me, it's home. #Mississippi

Alexis gassed up her car and headed towards Interstate 285. She was thrilled to be heading home but she sometimes dreaded the drive. It could be boring but she had a playlist and a few different audio books just in case. She always stopped at this one gas station in Birmingham, AL because it had all her favorite snacks: Boston baked beans, chico sticks, and laffy taffy, especially the banana flavor. She finally made it to her stopping point and just as she was exiting her car her phone rang. It was an unknown number and Alexis never answered unknown numbers, so she let it go to voicemail. Immediately, they called right back. Again, she didn't answer. Once again, the phone rang. Alexis picked up.

"Hello?"

There was just heavy breathing on the other end. So, she hung up the phone. Rolling her eyes, she went into the store. After getting her snacks and pumping her gas, Alexis grabbed her phone and looked at her notifications. She noticed that the unknown number called again twice and she also noticed she had notifications from her IG account, which wasn't uncommon when she posted her travel outfit. The first comment she saw was from Enrique. He wrote: 'you look gorgeous baby' with two white heart emojis. The next comment brought her out of her happy place quickly. Her creepy follower commented: How can I contact you outside of here? We need to talk.

Her body stiffen and her mouth went dry. She even noticed a slight tremble in her hands. Who was this person? Why would they need to talk with her? If Enrique saw this, he would lose his shit. She had a fleeting thought: maybe it was Remington. She quickly dismissed it, hoping he had better things to do than stalk her social media. He wasn't into social media when they were together. She can't imagine that had changed much with his new wife and baby. Surely, he would be focused on those new details in his life. She wrecked her brain trying to figure out if the date that Remington sent the flowers had any significance to their past relationship and she couldn't find any. None of it made sense.

Alexis finally arrived in Mississippi. She had run into traffic so she was rushing to get dressed to meet her sister for dinner in about an hour and a half. Of course, her mom was dressed. She still looked a little weak but there was definitely improvement since the last time Alexis was home. She and her mom sat at the kitchen table for a few moments chatting before she rushed off to her childhood bedroom to freshen up.

Dinner was full of laughs, hugs, and tears. Monica was so dramatic that it was funny. Momma was just happy to be feeling better and to have both of her girls with her.

"So, last week I received flowers," Alexis confessed.

"Enrique sent you 'just because' flowers?" Momma asked with a smile.

"Not quite. They were from Remington."

"What do you mean Remington?" Monica asked.

"Just what I said. I got home and thought Enrique sent flowers. I called him to thank him for the flowers and he said he didn't send them. I never read the card. Then I went back into the kitchen and saw Remington's signature black rose in the middle of the sunflowers."

"Why does he have your address and stuff like that?" Momma asked with way too much concern.

"All that information is public record, Momma," Monica responded. "But what is his fascination with black roses?"

"Enrique is upset and wants to come to Atlanta to have a conversation with him."

"Umm, I don't know if Enrique coming to Atlanta to chat with him is a good idea," Momma chimed in.

"I think it's a great idea. Where does he get off sending you flowers after the fiasco he had going on? Does he think flowers will change your mind? Where is his wife and new child?"

Alexis let out a sigh. She knew Monica would go off the deep end. She and Enrique were one in the same when it came to that. She was very overprotective. Alexis understood that was her role as her big sister but she could be brutal. Not saying that this situation didn't require serious assessment but there was no need for Enrique to fly to Atlanta to have a conversation that would not go well. Alexis could see how that would go south quickly.

"I have no answers to any of your questions. I can't figure out why he sent the flowers as I haven't had any contact with him in over a year."

"I don't like this, Alexis," Momma said.

"Yeah, it doesn't feel right. Be diligent and if you have to get a restraining order on him, do it. The audacity of him to look up your information and send some darn flowers. And why that black rose?" Monica asked again. "I always hated that he loved black roses so much."

"Yeah, the black rose was like his signature thing. I guess his way of being different," Alexis responded.

"He is definitely different. Touched even," Momma said.

All three of them burst into laughter. Alexis was relieved to have told them and to have the conversation out of the way. She just knew moving forward she would get a lot of questions about if he had reached out again. She really didn't need that from them and Enrique.

It was finally Friday and Alexis was headed to the Memphis airport to pick up Enrique. They hadn't talked much in the last few days. Honestly, she couldn't believe he was still pissy about her not letting him fly to Atlanta to ride down to Mississippi with her. The whole Remington and flowers thing had put a damper on their vibe. She didn't like that at all and they needed to have a conversation about it. As she sat in her car, she rehearsed different conversations in her head that she would have with Enrique about the whole ordeal.

Alexis looked up in just time to spot Enrique coming out of the airport. She hopped out of her car and ran up to him. She startled him just a bit but he recovered quickly. Pushing his luggage to the side, Enrique swooped her up in his arms before placing her back on her feet and placed a gentle kiss on her forehead. Once she was back on her feet, Enrique pulled her even closer to him and kissed her. He kissed her with so much passion and heat that Alexis' head was spinning. He pulled away and looked her in the eyes. He didn't say anything but he continued to stare at her. It wasn't a stare that made her uncomfortable but she did want to know what he was thinking.

"Well, hi to you too, Senor Manuel."

"Hey, my brown skin girl. You look fabulous."

"And you don't look too bad yourself." Enrique never took his eyes off Alexis. It began to make her self-conscious. "Why are you just staring at me like that?"

"Because you are mine. And you don't understand what that means."

"Umm, what does that mean?"

"Nothing that can't be discussed later. What's the plan for the day?"

"You don't get to do that, Enrique. Just change the subject."

"It really is a discussion for later but we will have it."

Alexis rolled her eyes. "Fine. We are going to check into the hotel and then we can meet Momma and Moncia for dinner later." Enrique burst into laughter and Alexis was confused. "What's so funny?"

"You. That southern accent gets really thick when you get back home with your folks. It's cute and I love it."

"Whatever. You want to drive or me?"

"I'll drive."

They rode to the hotel in silence. Alexis checked work emails and Enrique listened to his Spanish music from his playlist. There was tension and Alexis knew once they were settled into their room they would have a conversation. Probably one that she would want to avoid but Enrique would not let her. As they pulled into the parking lot of the hotel, Alexis let out a sigh. She didn't want a weekend that she had been anticipating to be overshadowed by Remington and his shenanigans.

Enrique grabbed their luggage out of the trunk. He stood at the back of the truck waiting for Alexis to get out. He knew she was intentionally moving slower than normal. He also knew she didn't want to be confrontational and would try to avoid the much-needed conversation. However, he had no intentions of avoiding the conversation but he would do it in a way in which she felt comfortable. Once they checked into the hotel, they headed up to the fifth floor.

The room offered an amazing view of Midtown Memphis. Alexis was excited about the balcony and hoped to enjoy a few minutes out there at some point during their stay. Enrique was a unpack your bag kind of guy while Alexis could definitely live out of her suitcase. Hell, she had done so when she was homeless after the breakup with Remington. Most people would say she wasn't homeless but she was according to the definition provided by the federal government. Anyway, she didn't have to be technical about it.

"What time are we meeting your mom and sister for dinner?"

"Umm, we have a few hours. I was thinking around seven o'clock."

"Good. We need to talk."

Alexis dreaded this part of relationships. She knew it was written all over her face, too. She didn't do a really good job of hiding her emotions. Before she could respond, she was already twisting on her hair. She let out another loud sigh.

"Fine. Let's talk."

"Hey, I'm not trying to pick a fight. I just want to understand you and help you understand me. I'm not actually thinking we need to talk. We can do an exercise."

"Huh? An exercise. What kind of exercise?"

"A writing exercise. As a writer, I know you express yourself better when writing." Enrique pulled two journals from his bag. He kept one for himself and gave her one. "I've already written some writing prompts for us to get started."

Alexis appreciated him being considerate but she was also nervous. He was correct; writing was the best way for her to express herself. She was really impressed with his willingness to go against the norm.

"Okay, so how does this work? Do we have the same writing prompts?"

"The first few pages will be the same but moving forward we can use the journal to express whatever we want but for now let's focus on completing the prompts already in the journal."

Alexis scanned the first few pages and noticed maybe four to five writing prompts. "Okay, this doesn't seem too bad."

"Great." Enrique smiled. "We'll write and share what we have written and then have a discussion."

"Sounds good. Thanks for doing it this way, too."

"Anything for you my brown skin girl."

Alexis smiled her big smile. She loved when he referred to her as his brown skin girl. It was one of her favorite compliments.

The first prompt read: What does a committed relationship look like to you?

Easy, Alexis thought. She began writing immediately. Her list began with things like: honesty at all times, spending quality time together, respecting each other, understanding one another, working through challenges, acknowledging and appreciating effort and so on. By the time she finished her list, Enrique was sitting there staring at her. She was in her zone. Writing was her thing.

"I'm done," Alexis announced.

"Good. Do you want to read them aloud or do you just want to swap journals?"

"Umm, we can just swap journals."

Alexis had grown anxious and self-conscious. She definitely didn't want him reading what she had written out loud. No matter how self-conscious she got she knew when she wrote out her emotions she didn't hold back so this exercise was definitely beneficial.

"Okay," Enrique agreed. They swapped journals and Alexis began reading.

A committed relationship is a relationship where two people mutually agree to openly communicate their feelings, respect each other and their differences, make an effort to be together, intentionally work to make each other happy, and be attentive to the other person's needs. In addition, for me, it means protecting what's mine at all times. And you, Alexis Carter, are MINE.

Alexis stared at the page. He made it so personal and very brief. She probably listed all the things she didn't get in her last relationship. Of course, all of it was hindsight when the shit hit the fan. In the midst of the relationship, she felt like the luckiest girl alive. She quickly thanked God for removing her from such a crazy situation.

Enrique looked up from reading to find Alexis staring at him. "I'm done. I'm a slow reader and you wrote a lot."

"It has more to do with you being a slow reader."

Enrique made his way over to Alexis who opted for sitting in the desk chair; whereas, he decided to sit on the bed. He stood in front of her and pulled her up. She obliged and laid her head on his chest. He kissed the top of head.

"You know you deserve more from a committed relationship."

"What do you mean?"

"You deserve someone who will protect you. Who will always be supportive of you. Who will encourage you to have these hard conversations. Who will always seek ways to make himself better for you and help you become a better woman, too."

His words and the movement of his hands up and down her arms soothed her. "I didn't know we were getting that deep. You didn't write a lot though."

"Because my commitment to you will always be to protect you, support you, acknowledge and appreciate your efforts, communicate honestly and openly, make you happy, and make sure your needs are met. My goal is to always remind you with actions why we chose each other. This is why the whole thing with your ex is a big deal to me."

"Thank you. I just don't want it to be an unnecessary thing if it doesn't have to be. I know how Remington is and things can go left really quickly. My best defense mechanism with him is to ignore him."

"For how long? Men like him don't stop at one thing. They keep going. He needs a hard stop to his foolishness."

"Can we at least see if it happens again before we go out in the deep end?"

"The last time was his last time, Alexis," Enrique said. "Look at me." Enrique gently touched her face. Alexis reared her head back slightly to look Enrique in the eyes. "I will not play about you. You need to understand that but most importantly your ex needs to understand that as well."

"What are you suggesting?"

Enrique grabbed Alexis' hands and looked in her eyes.

"I'm suggesting I come to Atlanta and have a conversation with him like a real man."

"How would we find him? It just seems like a lot."

"Stop saying that. Nothing is a lot when it comes to you. You know where his office is right?"

"I know where his old office is," Alexis said as she bit her lip. She felt her palms clam up. "I'm not sure if he's still there." Alexis wanted a way out of this mess and she needed to convince Enrique that him coming to Atlanta was unnecessary.

"Well, I'll just go by there and see if it's still his office. Hell, I can go to his house."

"Umm, can we just see if it happens again? If it happens again, I promise you'll be the first to know and then you can handle it however you see fit."

Enrique didn't respond immediately. He was giving serious thought to what Alexis requested. This was not his regular mode of operation. He didn't give anyone a chance to cross him more than once. But he knew for Alexis he would have to make a few compromises here and there.

"You have to promise me that if he so much as requests to follow you on social media that you will tell me. Any contact from him will warrant me having this conversation."

"I promise."

Alexis let her body relax against Enrique. He wrapped his arms around her and they stood in silence for a few moments. The moment was interrupted when his phone started ringing.

"That's my mom. I forgot to text her when I arrived." They broke apart and Enrique answered his phone. He spoke with his mom briefly before turning his attention back to Alexis. "Mom says hi and she can't wait to hang out in a couple of weeks when you come back to Austin."

"Your mom is really cool. And she seems to be able to keep you in line."

"Not really. I let her think so for her ego."

"Whatever, Mr. I do what I want."

"Not what I want but what I'm required to do. Keep that in mind."

"Umm, okay. I'm sure it was a hidden message in there."

"Nope. I said what I said." He winked and placed a kiss on her collarbone. "Right now, I'm required to help you ease the tension from the last week or so."

"Oh really? How are you going to do that?"

"By making love to you all over this hotel room and then tonight on the balcony."

Alexis should not have been anticipating the balcony promise as much as she was. Her body temperature rose a few degrees. "Let's start in the shower," she suggested.

"Say less," Enrique replied.

They giggled at his use of such a trendy phrase.

CHAPTER TWENTY-FOUR

Alexis and Enrique thoroughly enjoyed their time together in Memphis. It was always bittersweet when it was time for them to part ways. Dinner with her mom and sister had gone well. Of course, they loved him and when they spent time with him they fell even more in love. After Alexis dropped Enrique off at the airport on Sunday night, she went back to her mom's house.

"Lexie, I'm so happy for you."

"Thanks Mom. I can tell you really like Enrique, too."

"He's a good catch, baby. I mean you are a good catch, too, but he's crazy about you."

"You think so?"

"Child, a blind man can see that. I'm going to take it a step farther and say he's in love with you."

"That might be a little too far, Mom."

"Listen, I know a man in love when I see one. The way he looks at you is the same way your dad looked at me in the beginning."

"Awe, Momma. Do you miss him? I mean as your husband?"

"I miss what we had but I don't miss who he had become. I miss the loving, attentive man that captured my heart, not the workaholic that neglected me."

"I'm sorry, Momma. Do you think you will ever find love again?"

"Baby, I don't have to. The love your dad and I shared can last me a lifetime. He was my soulmate. Plus, I'm too old to be out here dating every Tom, Dick, and Harry."

"You're not too old, Momma. Besides, Daddy moved on so should you."

"Your daddy remarried. He didn't move on."

"What does that mean?"

"Nothing. This conversation is about you and Enrique. That boy loves you. You will see. Do me a favor and don't fight it."

"I won't. Can I be honest with you?"

"Always. That's our rule."

"I think I'm in love with him already. I may have come back from Spain in love with him."

"He probably felt the same way, too. Just know you are not in it alone."

"It's scary. The last time I thought I was in love. Well, you know how that ended."

"That damn boy was a fool. And I fault his momma for it. She didn't raise him well. He can't be too over you since he's sending flowers. Just be careful with that, okay?"

"Yes, ma'am. I had to calm Enrique down because he wants to fly to Atlanta to have a conversation with Remington."

"Again, that's love. He will always protect what's his. And he considers you his."

"Wait, have y'all been talking or something because he said the same thing."

"No, I just know what it's like to have a man to love like that."

"Can I ask you something?"

"As long as it's not about me and your dad."

"That's not fair, Momma. You know it's about that."

"We believe in honesty but there are just some things I'm not willing to discuss with you right now. I'm not saying never but not just right now."

"Okay, Momma."

"But don't be out here thinking that your dad and I are messing around because we are not. I wouldn't disrespect myself or another woman like that."

"I wouldn't dare think anything like that."

Deep down, Alexis was happy her mom cleared that up because she was starting to feel like she was keeping a deep, dark secret. She was happy to know it wasn't that. This was the first time her mom had been so candid about her feelings and relationship with her dad. It had to be difficult for her to sit around and not be with the love of her life. Her soulmate as she had put it. It actually made Alexis sad for her mom. Alexis was brought out of her thoughts at the sound of her mom's voice.

"So, when do you plan to tell Enrique about your feelings?"

"Not sure, I will. I don't want to tell him and then it's not mutual."

"Girl, the worst thing that will happen is you feel rejected but that shouldn't be a worry of yours. Trust me, he feels the same way."

"You seem so sure."

"And I am. That tall ass boy loves you. But play if you want. You will find out."

"It sounds like you are threatening me."

"Child, not at all. I'm just warning you, baby girl."

Alexis and her mom continued their conversation and at some point, it turned to all the gossip in town. Her momma knew everybody's business. Alexis was too tickled but she appreciated staying abreast of all the latest and greatest in her small hometown.

The next morning, Alexis headed back to Atlanta. She opted out of posting on social media over the weekend but she would upload pics from her weekend of fun. After she made the six-hour drive back to Atlanta and relaxed a bit, she started to plan her week. She decided to give Enrique a call but he didn't answer so she sent him a quick text.

Alexis: Just thinking of you, babe. *heart emojis*

Enrique: I miss your brown skin self. I miss kissing you all over. I miss making you moan my name in pleasure, too.

Alexis: Oh really? I just called you though.

Enrique: At the movies with mom. I'll call you when we leave here.

Alexis: Eww, you're talking to me like that sitting beside your mom. Gross *laughing emoji*

Enrique: I could be sitting beside Jesus and I would have said the same thing. I can tell you some more things I miss. Shall I?

Alexis: Enrique no. Enjoy the movie with your mom and call me later. *kissing emoji*

Enrique: *kissing emoji*

Alexis decided to make her social media post. It always came with so much anxiety. She didn't want to wake the sleeping creep that was her dedicated follower. She posted pics from the picnic she and Enrique had on the riverside and the journals he had gotten for them. She hadn't realized it was personalized until they were down on the riverside. They were getting ready to write from another prompt when Enrique asked her what she thought about the personalization. The leather journal was engraved and read: To the most beautiful brown skin girl I've ever met, MY Alexis Carter. -EM

Of course, Alexis swooned over the message. Her social media post read: A weekend well-spent. He gets me and for that I am grateful. It's a great feeling to be cared for so well.

Her first like was from her creepy follower. They also commented with three heart emojis. Alexis rolled her eyes and kept on with her day. She and Enrique talked later that evening and they both were excited about her flying back to Austin the upcoming weekend. It felt like it had been forever since they were together. It was also hard to believe they were coming up on their six month anniversary. Wow, it had been six months already.

A ringing phone interrupted the moment of euphoria. Alexis didn't recognize the number but she answered it anyway.

"Hello, this is Alexis." There was only jazz music playing in the background. "Hello?"

Still nothing from the caller. So, Alexis hung up the phone and blocked the number. She instantly thought about telling Enrique but she couldn't confirm it was Remington and she didn't need an unnecessary confrontation. The next couple of days she would continue to receive these weird phone calls from various numbers. She blocked all of them and even stopped answering at some point. Then they would just leave a long ass voicemail playing jazz music or some random R&B song. Alexis couldn't imagine Remington had time in his schedule to harass her like this but she couldn't think of anyone else who would want to bother her either. Or maybe it was Devontae's crazy ass. Nah, even with his craziness he wouldn't stoop this low. Plus, she hadn't heard from him in a couple of years.

It was the morning that Alexis was flying out to Austin. She posted her customary travel outfit but she also posted a pic of her on the MARTA train. The caption read: Train chronicles. Not sure why I decided to do this…Anyway, catching another flight. Already caught feelings. Ladies, we can do both. #flewedout *heart emojis*

Enrique was the first to like her post and he commented: Caught feelings? He's a lucky man. *heart emojis* The creepy follower hearted both her caption and Enrique's response. Alexis just rolled her eyes. It was so annoying and she couldn't think of any good reason to continue to have this person follow her account. They really did give off creepy vibes yet she listened to Amina and continued to let them interact.

The flight to Austin was short and Alexis had gotten really engrossed in writing in her journal. After her conversation with her mom, she had decided to start writing how she felt in her journal. She also knew Enrique would be reading it this weekend because that was the decision that they made to share their journal entries whenever they were together. Alexis wasn't as anxious to share but she had been very transparent and vulnerable in the majority of the entries. It wasn't even a guarantee that Enrique would read all of them because she had written a lot during their time away.

When her flight landed, she texted Enrique. After another fifteen minutes or so Alexis was exiting the airport. She stepped out and spotted him immediately. It was like his energy always pulled him to her even in a crazy crowd of people. He greeted her with a dozen sunflowers. The message wasn't lost on her. He wanted to erase the memory that Remington created.

"Hey baby, these are for you."

"Thank you. And of course, they are for me." They both laughed.

"How was your flight?"

"It was good. It's still early, can we stop by somewhere to get a caramel frappe?"

"Yes or I could just make you one when we get home."

"Umm, okay that sounds good. I just want a snack."

"And you're using a caramel frappe as a snack?"

"Yes, judge me not."

"Never judging."

Enrique leaned in and kissed Alexis before they headed for his truck. He put her luggage in the backseat and they drove off. Traffic was crazy. It wasn't quite rush hour but it was still pretty early in the morning. It took longer than usual to get to his condo. Alexis would never get over the fact that he designed and owned the building he was living in. It was mind boggling to her and he acted as if it was nothing.

Just as they entered the condo, Alexis' phone started ringing. She looked at the screen and didn't recognize the number. A look of worry must have flashed across her face because Enrique asked her if everything was okay.

"Umm, yeah. I've just been getting these weird calls for the last couple of weeks. The caller doesn't say anything, just plays jazz or a random R&B song in the background."

The anger that Alexis saw in Enrique's eyes when she looked up told her everything she needed to know.

"What do you mean the last couple of weeks, Alexis?"

"Just that. I didn't say anything because I can't prove that it's Remington so I didn't want to get you upset over nothing."

"If it's not him, who the hell else is it? Do you think it's a coincidence that he sends you those damn flowers and now you're getting calls from random numbers?" Enrique's jaw muscles flexed and his tone was harsher than what Alexis was used to.

Alexis noticed Enrique's grip on the steering got tighter. She could feel the anger permeating off of him. "It could be. I don't know. I just don't like how upset you get about this situation."

"Upset? You think this is upset? You are about to see a side of me you don't want to see. Yes, I get upset because you are being harassed by your sorry ass ex and you don't want me to intervene."

"I just don't think it's necessary at this point."

Enrique took a deep breath before responding to Alexis. She didn't think he would even respond after a few seconds of silence.

"Okay, help me understand at what point will it be necessary? When he does something to you? Shows up at your house? Kidnaps you? Then will it be necessary or too damn late?"

His voice was louder than he expected but his frustration was at an all-time high with Alexis.

"That all sounds extreme."

"Extreme? It's extreme that you're protecting this asshole when he is harassing you."

"I'm not protecting him. And you are really upset. You're raising your voice."

"You're right. I am really upset but I shouldn't be raising my voice. I apologize."

"Accepted."

"Alexis, listen to me. One of my biggest challenges is staying calm as it relates to protecting what's mine. You have to understand there is really no middle ground for me. Your ex is constantly making it known that he has a problem with staying in his lane."

"I appreciate you wanting to protect me."

"No, I'm going to protect you. Now, carry on with what you were about to say."

"I just don't feel like it is necessary right now."

Alexis' phone started ringing and Enrique gave her a questioning look. She nodded and handed him the phone. He answered, putting the call on speakerphone.

"Hello?" The jazz music was playing in the background. Suddenly, it stopped and Enrique said hello again. Then the call ended. "I guess the asshole was startled because I answered the phone."

"I guess so. Umm, do you mind fixing me some hot tea instead of the caramel frappe?"

"Are you okay?"

"Yes, I'm just a little tired and definitely didn't expect to start our visit fussing."

"We are not fussing. We are communicating."

"I'm going to take a quick shower so I can lay across the bed for a while and relax."

"Hey, come here," he said. Alexis walked into his arms. "I'm sorry. You're right, we need to be mindful of how we spend our time together but I'm not apologizing for being upset about this situation. I'll handle it differently moving forward though."

"Thank you."

Alexis placed small kisses on the inside of his forearm. She left the kitchen and headed to the bathroom to take a hot shower. She just needed a few minutes alone so she could mentally and emotionally recharge. It wasn't even ten o'clock yet and so much had transpired. She didn't want the weekend to be intense. After her shower, she lay across Enrique's California King bed in her pajama bottoms and tank top. Enrique entered the room with a cup of hot tea and his journal.

"Just in case you want to do some light reading while you relax."

She giggled. "Light reading huh? Mine is in my bag that I left downstairs on the kitchen island."

"I'll grab it. I'm heading into my office if you need me. Your phone is on the charger downstairs because of course it was on ten percent battery."

"Thank you. Hey, are we good?"

"We are better than good, my brown skin girl."

"Okay."

He leaned in and kissed her forehead and then made his way to her lips. The kiss intensified quickly and Alexis was expecting things to move in the direction of sex but Enrique broke the kiss and gave her a boyish grin.

"Not right now. You need to rest and I need to do a couple virtual meetings but when I'm done I'll be all yours."

"That's not fair."

"Life isn't fair."

Enrique left the room. Alexis sipped her hot tea and picked up his journal. She flipped to the entry from their last pre-written prompt and refreshed her memory before reading on to the next few entries. Surprisingly, he had written way more than she expected.

She wasn't sure how much time had passed before she finished reading about ten pages in his journal. She never got tired of reading his perfect handwriting. How he managed to write so neatly and in cursive was beyond her.

She sat still for a moment taking in all that she read. Enrique confessed his love for her. His responsibility to protect her. He was so big on protecting her and she couldn't help but wonder where this strong urge had come from. After reading his journal, she had no doubt that he was in love with her.

He spelled it out plainly. He would soon find out that she felt the same way once he had a chance to read her journal entries. He would also find out more about her last relationship and some of the fears that she carried with her from that. Alexis made an impromptu decision to head to Enrique's office but not before she changed into something sexier.

She rummaged through her luggage and pulled out a sexy red lingerie number. It was lace and crotchless. She smiled at her choice because she was certain this would get his attention. She would definitely be testing his self-control. If he was on a work call and could manage to still continue, she would be impressed. Honestly, she was hoping that he would find her irresistible and not be able to finish the call. She changed quickly, pulled her hair up, and put on some red lipstick. She opted out of the heels because she wasn't about to break her neck trying to navigate those damn steps that led to his office.

Alexis entered Enrique's office while he was mid-sentence. She stood in front of his desk with an innocent look as if she was casually wearing a sundress. Enrique never finished his sentence. Alexis then heard a voice say, "You look like you just saw a ghost. Everything okay, son?"

Oh shit, he's on the phone with his dad. Definitely bad timing, Alexis thought.

"Not a ghost, Dad. Can we table this discussion? Something more pressing has come up."

"Yes, but we need to get this finalized in the next couple of days. I don't want to miss this opportunity."

"And we won't. Give me about forty-five minutes and I promise we will get this finalized and move on to the next project."

"Sure, son. You are definitely distracted. Talk to you later."

"Bye, Dad." Enrique ended the video chat and wasted no time making his way around his desk to me.

"I'm sorry. I didn't know you were on the phone with your dad."

"Woman, hush. I could've been on the phone with Jesus and I would've gotten off."

Alexis giggled because he was always making a reference to Jesus and what he would have done in his presence.

He pulled her close to him and assessed the outfit. The heat in his eyes told the story. He pinched her nipples through the thin lace material. He brought his mouth closer to her breast and nibbled at her right breast while still pinching the left one. Alexis noticed it was painful but pleasurable as well. He continued this torture for a couple more minutes and then he guided Alexis over to one of the chairs in his office. He commanded for her to bend over. Before long, she could hear his zipper and felt him shedding his pants and boxer briefs. Then she heard the infamous tearing of the foil packet. That sound had become one of her favorite sounds with Enrique. She knew that was the beginning of pleasurable sounds.

CHAPTER TWENTY-FIVE

Alexis was on cloud nine after a very memorable weekend with Enrique. After this weekend, she felt they had grown closer. Of course, they had amazing sex but the intimacy was different than what they shared previously. Something definitely shifted in their relationship. She also knew he was serious about her allowing him to protect her.

She was in la la land on the MARTA headed to the train station where she parked her truck. Her phone rang and it was an unknown number. She declined the call. She didn't want anything to get her out of her great mood. Of course, it rang again. Alexis declined the call again. This continued for the next four to five minutes. She finally put her phone on silent and headed towards her car. It was still early in the day with plenty of daylight. When she was about twenty feet from her car, she stopped in her tracks. Broken glass was all around her truck.

She couldn't believe someone had broken into her car. How did security let this happen? She walked up to her car to inspect the damage. Not only did someone break her truck windows but three of her tires had been flatten. What the hell? Alexis stood in disbelief. As if on cue, she spotted a security guard making his way to her car.

"Hi ma'am. Is this your vehicle?"

"Umm, yes. How the hell did this happen?"

"I'm not sure. A lady reported it on her way out a few minutes ago."

"So, this just happened?"

"It had to have just happened. We make our rounds regularly and this wasn't like this an hour ago."

"What the hell? Do y'all have surveillance?"

"Yes, we do. My co-worker is running the cameras back now. I already contacted MARTA police so you can file a report."

"Thank you. I need to find a tow truck after this."

Alexis tried her hardest to sound as unbothered as possible but she was pissed. This definitely didn't seem like something Remington would do but who else would do something like this? Was it her creepy follower on IG? That's it. She was deleting that page. She took a deep breath but she knew she needed to call Enrique. Maybe she would call him after she had spoken with the police officers. She looked down at her phone and saw she had a message from him.

Enrique: I miss you already, brown skin girl. Let me know when you get home and settled.

Alexis: I miss you, too. I wish I was back there already.

And that was the truth. Being in his presence made her feel protected, seen, and loved. Being back in Atlanta dealing with dumb shit like this was not what she expected. Soon the MARTA police arrived and they went through the customary paperwork and asked questions like if she had any idea who may have done this. For some odd reason, Alexis' gut was telling her this was not something Remington would do. She simply answered, "no."

The security guard stayed with her while she waited for a tow truck. While she waited, she contacted her insurance company. They asked her to take pictures which she had already done. She was avoiding the phone call to Enrique. She would do that once she got home. It took the tow truck forever to arrive. Once it did, she called an Uber to take her home. Once she got home, she took a hot shower in hopes of easing her stress. She then fixed a cup of hot tea. She took out her phone and sent Enrique a text message.

Alexis: Apparently, someone had nothing better to do.

She then attached the photos she had taken earlier. She didn't get an immediate response. A few more minutes went by and she still hadn't received a response. He must have been busy. She stretched out on her sectional in her living room and started to doze off. Her phone began ringing. Alexis begrudgingly answered. She didn't bother looking at the caller ID. All she heard was jazz music. She decided to try something different.

"Look, you're calling my phone repeatedly and not saying anything. You can make your presence known or continue to be a coward."

That was enough for the person on the other line to end the call. She hoped it was enough for them to stop calling her damn phone, too. The shit was getting ridiculous. Alexis decided to call her mom and sister on a conference call so she would only have to tell the story once. Of course, neither one of them were convinced that it wasn't Remington. She just couldn't see him doing something like that. She also didn't think he was capable of living a double life yet he did. Maybe she was giving him too much credit.

After she ended the call with her mom and sister, she decided to loop Brooklyn, Reign, and Justice into the bullshit taking place. She sent them a text message with the same images that she had sent to Enrique. They all shared the same concern and were in agreement with her sister and mom that it could be Remington. Hell, they all thought it was him.

She knew someone would ask what Enrique said about the situation since she told them how pissy he had gotten before about the flowers and phone call. Of course, it was Brooklyn's ass that asked.

Alexis: He hasn't responded yet. He may be spending time with his mom since we didn't see her much this weekend.

Justice: Or he may be on a flight to Atlanta.

Reign: Ditto that.

Brooklyn: If he is, that's your damn husband bih…

Alexis shook her head. Leave it up to Brooklyn.

Alexis: I doubt he's on his way to Atlanta. He has a lot of big meetings this week that require his undivided attention.

Justice: Okay.

Brooklyn or Reign didn't chime in but Justice got her thinking. What if he was on his way? This could turn into a whole mess. Alexis decided to call his phone. It had been a couple hours since she had sent the text messages.

He answered on the first ring, "Hello, Alexis."

Relieved that he had answered his phone but also confused by his greeting and by the fact that he hadn't called after he received her text message.

"Hey. I texted you earlier. Did you get my message?"

"I sure did."

"Umm, okay..." Enrique didn't say anything more and it was an awkward silence. "Are you upset with me?"

"No. Not upset. Irritated."

"Why?"

"You sent me a text message of your vandalized car like the sh.. like it's normal. You didn't call."

"I sent the text message when I got home and I was going to call once I got settled and was able to regroup. I needed some

time to just think but when you didn't
respond to my text message I figured you
were busy. So, I was waiting for you to call
me back when you were available."

"Too busy for you, Alexis? When is that ever
a thing?"

"I just didn't want to bother you if you were
spending time with your mom."

"Okay, well I'm busy now and I actually
need to go. I'll talk to you in a few."

"Umm, okay."

Alexis ended the call. Her grip on her phone
was tighter than she realized. She relaxed
her grip a little. She just didn't understand
him. One minute he was saying he was
never too busy for her and the next minute
he was busy and needed to get off the
phone. If she was being honest with herself,
her feelings were hurt. They had such a
great weekend and now this. She decided
to do something she hadn't done in a while.
She went upstairs in her office, searching
for her coloring book and coloring pencils.
She found the perfect image and started
coloring. Once she finished that page, she
started coloring another. In her haste to
leave from downstairs, she left her phone.

She jumped when she heard her doorbell
ring. It was well after nine o'clock. Who
would be at her door this time of the night?

She instantly went on alert. She went into her bedroom and grabbed her gun out of her nightstand. Her hands shook as she made her way downstairs. She was halfway down the stairs when her doorbell rang again. Damn, she should have grabbed her phone so she could look at her ring camera. Finally, she made it to the living room and grabbed her phone. She pulled up the ring camera and the biggest smile spread across her face. She laid her phone and gun on the kitchen island as she headed to the door.

When she opened the door she found a very disgruntled Enrique. He had parked his rental car in the driveway.

"Hey. I won't even ask why you're here because I know the answer to that." He pulled her into his arms and kissed the top of her forehead. He didn't say anything. "Do you want to park the rental in the garage?"

"Absolutely not." He continued into the house. Alexis trailed behind him after locking the door and setting the alarm.

"Why didn't you have the alarm set at first?"

"I usually set it right before I go to bed."

"Hell, I thought you were in bed since you weren't answering your phone and it took you so long to answer the door."

"No, I was upstairs coloring."

"Coloring?" Enrique asked with a raised brow.

"Yes, coloring. I do that sometimes to relax."

"Oh, you're stressed? I can't tell."

"Are you going to be an asshole the entire time you're here because I don't need that."

"You're right. I apologize. I just need you to see how frustrating it is that you aren't taking this situation seriously."

"What situation? I can't say it was Remington that vandalized my car. Honestly, I don't think it was him."

"You give him too much credit. I guess we will find out tomorrow when I pay him a visit."

"Enrique, is that necessary?"

"Alexis, yes it's necessary. Again, I will protect what's mine at all times and you are mine."

Alexis rolled her eyes. "I haven't eaten dinner and I'm hungry so I'm going to cook something really quick."

"I'll have whatever you are having." They made their way into the kitchen. Enrique spotted the gun on the kitchen island. He walked over and picked it up. "Are you downplaying the situation, Alexis? Why is this out?"

"It's out because someone popped up at my house unannounced at almost ten o'clock on a Sunday night."

"Would a Friday or Saturday night have been better?" Alexis was just about to get pissed but she noticed the slight smile that touched his lips. "Come here. I can't stay mad at you too long but I do plan to get to the bottom of this while I'm here and I'm not leaving until I do."

"I thought you had important meetings all week?"

"Nothing is as important as you, my brown skin girl. I really mean that when I say that. I'm going to freshen up while you cook."

"Okay."

Alexis was over the moon excited that Enrique was there. She felt a sense of relief but she was also nervous about him confronting Remington. She pulled out her phone and sent a quick text message to her girls' group with Justice, Brooklyn, and Reign.

Alexis: Justice was spot on. Enrique showed up a few minutes ago.

Justice: Good night. I knew he would.

Brooklyn: Yes, I'll be a bridesmaid.

Reign: Good. I'm happy he's there. And I'm a bridesmaid too, bih...

Alexis: Hush. Ain't no bridesmaids. I'm happy he's here, too. I'm a little nervous because he wants to have a conversation with Remington.

Brooklyn: Awe, shit. This could get wild.

Justice: Enrique won't let it get too crazy. I'll be the Matron of Honor though. *laughing emoji*

Reign: Somebody needs to talk to Remington's punk ass. He needs to tend to his wife and kids.

Brooklyn: Exactly. How long is Enrique there for?

Alexis: I don't know. He said as long as he needs to be.

Justice: This could be very interesting.

Alexis and Enrique enjoyed a quick dinner of spinach and ricotta cheese ravioli covered in marinara sauce and parmesan cheese and grilled Brussel sprouts. They ate in silence. There was still some tension and Alexis wished it would just vanish. After such a wonderful weekend all of this had to happen.

"What's the plan for tomorrow?" Alexis asked.

"I'm going to Remington's office tomorrow and if he's not in I'll wait for him to show up. After that, I'll go check on your car and how long it will take to be repaired."

"What time did you want to go to his office? I have a few calls in the morning."

"You're not going with me, Alexis. No disrespect but I don't want him to be graced with your presence. I can't imagine you want to see him anyway."

"Umm, I just don't want things to get out of control. I feel like both of you can be hot heads."

"Nah, I'm always level-headed."

"Not with me you aren't."

"I am level headed *with* you but I won't compromise on your safety."

Alexis rolled her eyes and started to gather the dishes to load the dishwasher. Enrique grabbed her as she got close to him. He stood and looked down at her. He cupped her face and kissed her passionately. There was a sense of desperation in his kiss. He finally pulled back and Alexis sighed in disappointment.

"You are my world. You are my priority. Your safety is my responsibility, Alexis. When you realize that, my actions will start to make more sense to you."

CHAPTER TWENTY-SIX

Alexis tossed and turned most of the night. Enrique knew it was because she was nervous about him meeting her ex tomorrow. What she didn't know was he knew just enough information on Remington Slayton to keep him away from his woman forever. He was certain Remington wouldn't put up a fight. If he had any sense, he wouldn't.

It was a little after nine o'clock when Enrique left the next morning. He hadn't bothered to take the manila envelope out of the car the night before. He didn't want to run the risk of Alexis asking questions because he didn't want to share the information with her. He didn't want her to know what kind of narcissistic psycho she had been involved with. Enrique dressed in his usual white t-shirt that hugged his upper body, jeans that showed off his muscular thighs, and his casual shoes. He had his curls pulled back into a ponytail. He knew Alexis particularly enjoyed the five o'clock shadow that he wore. He also knew her nerves were all over the place as they sat together and had breakfast. He saw the tension in her shoulders. She sighed several times and her focus seemed to be all over the place. She had to trust him and he would prove just how trustworthy he was. Enrique wasn't the least bit bothered. He was so sure that Remington wouldn't put up a fuss. He couldn't tell Alexis why he was so sure. If he shared the information he had, it would only make Alexis have more questions. He didn't need that.

Just as Enrique was headed out the door, Alexis' phone began ringing. Enrique gave her a knowing look as if to ask if it was the unknown number. Alexis nodded her head. He answered the phone. As soon as his voice registered with the caller, there was a dial tone. For some reason, they didn't like when he answered the phone. He waited a couple more minutes to see if the caller would call back but they didn't.

Enrique arrived at Slayton's graphics in less time than he had expected. He noticed there were two cars parked out front, a red BMW and a black Cadillac Escalade. He pulled into the spot next to the red BMW and exited his vehicle. He was greeted by a vibrant younger girl.

"Welcome to Slayton graphics. Do you have an appointment?"

"No, I don't but I'm here to see Remington."

"Umm, Mr. Slayton only takes appointments on Mondays."

"This is a pressing matter and I'm sure his schedule can accommodate it."

"I'll see. What's your name?"

"Enrique Manuel."

The girl disappeared from the front desk and headed down the hall. Moments later, she reappeared with Remington.

"Mr. Manuel, Brittany might have informed you that I only take appointments on Mondays. She said you were insistent so I thought I might come see what the urgent matter is."

Enrique didn't bother greeting Remington or anything. He politely handed him the envelope. "I'm sure you'll have a few minutes to spare."

Remington opened the envelope and after glancing through the first few documents his body tensed. "What is this in regard to Mr. Manuel?"

"Alexis Carter."

"Alexis?"

"Yes, *my* Alexis Carter. Shall we speak in private?"

"Absolutely. Brittany, will you block off an hour on my calendar and reschedule my ten o'clock appointment?"

"That won't be necessary. What I have to say will only take a few minutes. I don't need a lot of your time." Enrique followed Remington the short distance to his office where Remington hurriedly closed the door.

"How did you get these documents?"

"I have connections. Your secret is safe with me though. I have one demand. Stay away from Alexis Carter. Absolutely no contact. No more harassing phone calls. No more flowers. No more stalking her IG page. And I pray to God you weren't responsible for vandalizing her car yesterday."

"Someone vandalized her car?"

The way he asked the question led Enrique to believe Remington but you couldn't trust a man like Remington. His whole life was built on lies.

"Yes. Again, I pray it wasn't you because there will be consequences for whoever did this."

"Man, look I sent flowers but I haven't been calling her, stalking her social media, and damn sure didn't vandalize her car. That wouldn't be smart for a guy that was looking for a second chance." The glare that appeared on Enrique's face made Remington begin to stumble over his words. "Was. That was until I found out she had someone. I understand she's off limits."

"Great, have the day you deserve."

Enrique left Remington's office and he was certain that would be the end of that bullshit. There was a lingering question though. If Remington wasn't behind the social media stalking, phone calls, and car vandalism then who the hell was?

Enrique spent a total of ten days in Atlanta. He ensured Alexis' car was fixed properly. They hadn't figured out the social media stalking, phone calls, or who vandalized her car because the cameras didn't show a clear picture of the individual. Of course, he hated to leave Alexis. He enjoyed sharing space with her and learning her daily routine. The intimacy was his favorite part of the day. They did a lot together. They worked out. They cooked together. He watched movies and watched her sleep because she never finished a movie. He finally got to hang out with her friends and meet Corey, Justice's husband. What started out as a not so good situation had actually worked in his favor. Everything about Alexis Carter said she was meant to be in his life. He couldn't wait to make that a permanent thing.

CHAPTER TWENTY-SEVEN

Alexis tossed and turned all night. She had grown so used to Enrique being there that it didn't feel right without him. She was slowly dragging the next morning. She had several meetings and promised Brooklyn and Reign that they would have dinner. After she forced herself out of bed, she decided to take a quick run around the neighborhood in hopes of getting the boost of energy she needed. She only had time for two miles. She headed out and she noticed a black sedan parked at the entrance to her subdivision. The car just seemed out of place. She had never seen it before but she kept running. When she returned the vehicle was gone. Alexis let out a sigh of relief. Honestly, she shouldn't have anything to worry about. She made it home, dressed quickly, grabbed breakfast, and headed out of the door.

The day went by way too fast for Alexis. She rushed home to change clothes to meet Brooklyn and Reign at their favorite Caribbean restaurant. She was craving jerk salmon and Rasta pasta. Alexis made it home in record time from midtown Atlanta. It was the time of the year where it got dark earlier so it always made it seem later than it really was. As she was upstairs getting dressed, she heard a loud shattering noise. She ran downstairs to see a brick had been thrown through her window. It was the kitchen window facing the rear of her house. Frantic. She grabbed her phone and dialed 9-1-1. She quickly gave the operator the details and was told an officer was being dispatched. Afterwards, she called Reign.

"Hey, Lexie. Are you headed over?"

"No. Can you get to my house ASAP?"

"What's going on? Yes, I'm on my way." At this point, Alexis was in tears. "Alexis, what's wrong? Is your mom okay?"

"Someone just threw a brick through my kitchen window!"

"What the hell? Did you call the police?"

"Yes, they are on their way."

"Okay, I'm on my way. I'll call Brooklyn so she can meet us over there, too. Do you want me to call Justice so she can have Corey come by?"

"Umm, I don't know."

Alexis was sobbing and Reign could barely make out what she was saying. "Okay, we will figure that out later. Call Enrique. I'm on the way."

That was the last thing Alexis wanted to do. She didn't want to bother him yet again with some of her bullshit. Who would want to throw a brick through her window? Better yet, how did they get into the complex if they didn't live there? *Oh my God, what if the creepy social media stalker lives in the same neighborhood and they've been watching me this entire time? What the fuck? This is crazy!* She didn't want to but she knew if she didn't call Enrique, all hell would break loose with him and she didn't need any more drama in her life. So, she got herself together and dialed his number.

"Hey, my brown skin girl."

"Hi."

"Hey, what's wrong? Don't say nothing because I can hear it in your voice."

"Umm, someone threw a brick through my kitchen window about five minutes ago."

"Alexis, what the hell?"

"I'm fine. I've called the police and Reign's on her way over here."

"I will catch the next flight out."

"Enrique. You don't have to. I'm fine. I promise."

"You don't sound fine and I really need to get to the bottom of this. I know it better not be Remington's punk ass."

"Will you please calm down?"

"Calm down? I'm hours away from you and someone is harassing you. How do you expect me to stay calm?"

"Look, the cops just arrived. I'll talk with them and then give you a call back. Please do not hop on a flight. Promise me you won't."

"I can't make that promise. I'll wait for your phone call."

Enrique hung up before Alexis could say anything else. It was like he was mad at her. She was damned if she did and damned if she didn't. She let out a big sigh and opened the door for the cops. They went through the regular questions. They even asked to look at her ring camera which didn't pick up anything since it was the rear of the house. Reign pulled up while the cops were still there. Alexis loved her friend but she knew she would have a thousand questions and her own narrative of who it was. The cops didn't spend too much time there.

Alexis was thankful that Justice sent Corey over and he patched the window as best as he could until she could get someone to come out. Alexis was making it a priority to get cameras installed around the perimeter of her property. Her townhome was an end unit. She was disappointed that her ring camera hadn't picked up any activity.

Brooklyn finally arrived with takeout from the restaurant. Of course, she did. That's who she was and Alexis couldn't be any more grateful at this moment.

"Thank you so much, Brooklyn," Alexis said.

"Of course, we weren't going to starve while we figure this shit out," Brooklyn responded.

"Honey, Enrique will be here shortly to figure it out. We are just moral support," Reign replied.

"Y'all, I hope he doesn't hop on a flight to come out here again. This is so embarrassing. I'm not sure who would even do this," Alexis said.

At that moment, she realized how exhausted she was. From not sleeping the night before to all of this right now, she was tired. Not just physically tired but mentally and emotionally drained. At this very moment, she wanted to ball up in her bed and cry. Alexis was brought out of her thoughts at the sound of Brooklyn's voice.

"I have a suspect in mind but I'll keep my thoughts to myself right now," Brooklyn said.

"Hell, you have said it now. So, who?" Reign asked.

Before Brooklyn could answer, Alexis' phone began ringing. It was Enrique's ringtone. She stepped out of the kitchen to answer the phone.

"Hey, babe. You didn't call back so I figured I would check in to make sure you are okay."

"Yes, sorry. Reign showed up then Brooklyn showed up with food so we were eating. Corey came by and patched the window the best he could."

"I know you're not staying there tonight."

"I would like to but I know I shouldn't. I'll check into a hotel for a couple of days. I'm getting cameras installed around the perimeter of the house and I'll get someone out to repair the window tomorrow, hopefully."

"Great, sounds like you have it all taken care of. Let me make your hotel reservation."

"You don't have to do that."

"I know I don't have to but I want to. Don't fight me on it. I'll send you the email confirmation shortly. Let me know when you are leaving your house and heading to the hotel."

"Okay, thanks. Hey, I love you. You know that right?"

"Do you really?" Enrique chuckled before saying, "I kind of figured as much though. I hope you know I love you, too. Way more than you can imagine."

"Yeah, I do know that. I'll call you when I leave the house."

"Bye, my brown skin girl."

Alexis stood still and just took in the moment. There was a lightness that took over her after that very short conversation. She knew that no matter what was happening in her life that was beginning to resemble a lifetime movie again, she would always come back to Enrique for peace and balance.

When she entered the room her demeanor had changed and she had more pep in her step.

"Damn, that phone conversation must have been amazing," Brooklyn said.

"Cause baby you came around that corner walking like a new woman," Reign chimed in.

"Yeah, I just told Enrique that I loved him and I do…" Alexis said.

She didn't get a chance to finish her sentence because both Brooklyn and Reign started talking. One was saying it was about damn time and the other was asking why she told him over the phone. All three burst into laughter. Alexis was still tired as hell but she didn't feel as depleted. Enrique was what she needed on her worst days and this was a bad day. She longed to feel his body next to hers. She craved his touch. She was desperate to taste his lips. She needed him in ways she couldn't imagine. She would surprise him with a trip to Austin next weekend.

Alexis, Brooklyn, and Reign finished eating their food. They went upstairs while Alexis packed bags for her hotel stay. They were finally exiting her neighborhood and Alexis noticed the black sedan from earlier sitting in the same spot. She called Reign and let her know it was the same car. Reign said she circled back and got the license plate number. It wasn't a coincidence that the same vehicle was there.

Alexis called Enrique enroute to the hotel and gave him an update on the black sedan from earlier. Of course, he requested the license plate number so he could do his own digging. Once she was in the hotel, she showered and relaxed. She wrote in her diary and then she fell asleep. She was awakened by rustling in her room. Panic filled her. She was scrambling for the light when she heard his voice.

"Hey, babe it's me. It's okay."

"Oh my God, what are you doing here?" She was still visibly shaking.

"You should know me well enough by now to know that I was coming to you. I caught a late flight out."

"Of course, you did."

"Well, don't sound so excited."

"I'm always excited to see you but I wish you would stop dropping everything and running to my rescue. I handled everything this time."

"Alexis Carter." Enrique sat on the edge of the bed and pulled her into his arms. "Look at me. Alexis Carter, you are my priority. I will cross oceans, deserts, valleys, and walk on hot coals to make sure you are always safe and happy."

"It's just a lot. I know you didn't sign up for all of this. Hell, I didn't sign up for all of this."

"Yet here we are. It's teamwork. I'm here. I will always be here."

Alexis let her head fall softly into his chest while Enrique caressed the side of her face with his thumb. She couldn't deny the sense of relief she felt in his arms but she didn't like the role of damsel in distress either. She was grateful that he was showing her that she was his priority. She repositioned her body so that she was straddling him.

"Whoa, this can go left really quick, Alexis."

"Or it can go right. The verbiage doesn't matter."

"Okay, can I at least take a shower?"

"Only if I can join you."

"Of course."

Enrique stood with Alexis still wrapped around his waist. He carried her over to the bathroom and sat her on the countertop while he stripped naked. Alexis admired the masterpiece before here. It was after 1 AM and her phone started ringing. She jumped at the sound of her ringing phone. Enrique crossed the room in a lot fewer steps than she would have and answered. It was her alarm company letting her know that her alarm was going off. They let the representative know to dispatch the police. Before long, Enrique was putting his clothes back on and Alexis was dressing just as quickly. They were headed to Alexis' house. The sinking feeling she felt got worse the closer they got.

When Enrique finally pulled into her neighborhood there were flashing lights and three cop cars in her driveway. The officers checked the premises and didn't see anyone but her backdoor had been kicked off the hinges. From a quick glance around, nothing was taken. Alexis could feel the anger permeating off Enrique. She, on the other hand, was visibly shaking and wrecking her brain on who could be behind this. Surely, it was a man because what woman had enough strength to kick a door off its hinges? Was this Remington's doing? Or was the social media creep upset that she had deleted them? Nothing was making sense. Alexis did give the police officers the license plate for the black sedan she had seen in the neighborhood earlier.

After the police left, she and Enrique stood in the kitchen staring at each other.

"I'll figure all this out in the morning. In the meantime, I'll grab your tools and get this door put back on."

"Thanks."

That was all Alexis managed to say. The exhausting feeling returned with a vengeance. She wanted nothing more than to sleep for hours with no interruption. She would also like to wake up and realize this was all a bad dream.

Enrique found Alexis standing in the same spot that he had left her a couple minutes ago. He knew she wasn't okay so he wouldn't ask the dumb question, but he would make sure to get to the bottom of this nonsense. His first stop in the morning was to pay another visit to Remington because if he found out he was behind this bullshit he would turn his world upside down. He had given the cops his number to call him with information on the black sedan but he had already texted his private investigator to run his search. His guy wouldn't have information until morning since he was certain he was asleep right now.

After the door was fixed, they left for the hotel. They rode in silence as Alexis just stared out the window. Enrique reached over and grabbed her hand. He decided to let her be in that moment because nothing he would say was going to make her feel better. When they arrived at the hotel Alexis headed to the bathroom and turned the shower on.

"Come, join me please," she said.

"Of course."

Enrique stripped out of his clothes but with less excitement this time. They entered the shower and he stepped back. One thing he had learned about Alexis was that she enjoyed her water steaming hot. She stood under the water, careful not to get her hair wet. He watched as her shoulders relaxed. Enrique slowly walked behind her and she let her back fall into his chest. They stood like this for several minutes.

It wasn't long before they were making love. The moment felt so vulnerable. Call him crazy but he could feel Alexis surrendering herself to him. He didn't take it lightly. She was making it clear that she needed him. It was evident in the way she gave her body to him. He felt her relax underneath his touch and he appreciated the trust she was giving him. She held him a lot longer and tighter than normal.

Enrique was awake before Alexis. They had finally gone to sleep a little after 4 AM. Four hours later, he was up. He had actually gotten up after he heard his text notification. He dressed quickly to step into the hallway to speak with his private investigator.

"Hey, Watson. What's up? What ya' find?"

"Hey Manuel. The tag for the black sedan is a rental but it's rented to Remington Slayton."

"What the fuck? This asshole."

"That's not it though."

"What else is it?

"He's not in town. I confirmed that he's in California with his family for a family vacation. I sent videos to your email from his social media and his sister's social media."

"Man, what the fuck is going on here? Who the hell has he paid to harass Alexis?"

The anger Enrique felt was inexplicable. He knew his private investigator would be all over the situation, but he needed to know what the hell was going on now. And he would find out even if it meant him flying out to California and breaking up that little family vacation. He needed to find a way to send a clear message to Remington. He took a few minutes to come up with a plan.

CHAPTER TWENTY-EIGHT

Enrique spent more than a week in Atlanta. Alexis' door had been repaired, window fixed, and cameras were installed around her home. Enrique also had motion security lights installed as well. Initially, Alexis wanted to argue that it was overboard but she really did feel a lot better about the situation. Enrique also had another conversation with Remington and he swore he had nothing to do with the black sedan being parked in Alexis' neighborhood. He wasn't aware of any rentals and no one who had access to his information rented a vehicle. Enrique wasn't sold on it but he dropped it for the time being.

It had been three months since a brick had been thrown through her kitchen window and her back door had been kicked in. Alexis was convinced that Enrique had ties with the CIA or FBI because the information he was able to get his hands on was unbelievable. Honestly, Alexis was still in shock that Remington's wife, Nicole, was behind the social media stalking, phone calls, vandalizing her car, and all the stuff that had taken place at her house. It had to be something fundamentally wrong with her. She got the man that she wanted so badly but that wasn't enough for her. She still wanted to make Alexis' life miserable because Remington wasn't the shiny, gold trophy she thought he would be.

Three months earlier…

Enrique still would not give her the details of Remington's background but he assured her that she had been blessed to have cut ties with him when she did. Whatever it was that Enrique had on Remington was enough for him to stay quiet and out of her way. Once the private investigator had given Enrique the update, he started following the black sedan that was once again parked in the neighborhood. It wasn't long before they discovered it was a female driving the vehicle.

Alexis had had enough. She convinced Enrique that it was safe for her to confront the woman driving the car. Alexis approached the car with caution but she also had a 22 pistol in her pocket. If whoever this was decided to get crazy, she was ready to get crazy as well. Alexis noticed the person shift in the car as she approached. Enrique was not in sight and she wouldn't be able to leave too quickly as she had to wait for the gate to lift.

The closer Alexis got to the car, she realized it was a familiar face. Nicole's crazy ass. Alexis made it to the window and she thought Nicole would have tried to drive off but she didn't. Alexis tapped on the window for her to roll it down. Surprisingly, she obliged.

"What the fuck, Nicole? You're really stalking me?"

"You think you have such a perfect life, don't you?"

"What are you talking about? You got who you wanted…Remington. Hell, you even got the baby and the house. That's not enough? What else do you want from me?"

Nicole went on this tangent about how she was unhappy with Remington and wished she would have left him where he was. She didn't like how Alexis was happy and living her life.

"You need help. You know that right. You got the man you wanted. You got the child you wanted. You got the marriage you wanted. You got the house you wanted. And you're still so fucking unhappy that you stalk me."

"You make all your perfect posts and I'm stuck with the cheating bastard."

"Woe is me. You know the old saying how you get him is how you lose him. Take that into consideration."

"And I know he wishes I was you. He has said it a few times. He calls out for you in his sleep. How do I compete with that?"

"You don't. You leave. You deserve better than that. Just like I did."

Alexis was surprised by how calm she was now. Something about the look on Nicole's face told her she was desperate for a solution. And that was something Alexis couldn't help her with.

Nicole sat there with tears in her eyes. "It's something about your posts that triggers me; yet intrigues me. I am miserable Alexis and honestly, I wanted you to be just as miserable. I'm living in your shadows every day. Remington doesn't spend time with me. Just him and his kids. Even now, he's on family vacation and didn't bother to invite me. It's always him, RJ, and the twins. Even the girls still ask about you." Alexis was not sure how to respond to Nicole. She really felt sorry for her. At that moment, Enrique walked up to the car. Nicole tried to gather herself in his presence. Alexis noticed a fleeting look on Nicole's face. *This bitch cannot be serious because I will fuck her up about this one. He is NOT Remington.*

Nicole stopped talking and gave her undivided attention to Enrique.

"Hey babe, is everything okay here?"

Before Alexis could respond, Nicole responded, "Yes, it is fine." Alexis wasn't sure what kind of spell Enrique had her under but once she saw him, she never took her eyes off of him. It was unnerving but quite sad, too. Alexis was sure Nicole was used to getting attention from most men but Enrique never looked in her direction. Yet, another defeat for her to take back home with her. She hoped she didn't think she could take him from her.

"Look Nicole. I can't help you with the Remington problem."

"Wait, you know who this is?" Enrique quizzed.

"This is Remington's wife, Nicole Slayton."

"She's the one who has been following you, harassing you on social media, and countless other things?"

Alexis could hear the anger in Enrique's voice but she also saw it on his face. Nicole still sat staring at Enrique. It was clear she wasn't in her right mind.

"Yes, but we have come to an understanding that all of that stops today, right Nicole?"

"Sure."

That was all Nicole mustered up. It was like she was shell shocked by the looks of Enrique. Alexis knew it had to be difficult for her to watch their interaction when her life was falling apart. Part of Alexis felt sorry for Nicole but part of her rejoiced that she was getting some karma from the drama that she had caused in her life more than a year ago.

Alexis just hoped Nicole got the help she needed because her ass definitely needed help. She was charged with several crimes but Alexis really didn't want to press charges. It was clear she was suffering from mental health issues. Alexis got a restraining order against both Nicole and Remington but she didn't think Remington would be a problem. It was just a precaution and she knew it made Enrique feel better.

Chapter Twenty-nine

Alexis and Enrique managed to spend every weekend together. They would meet up in random cities for date nights or weekends or spend the weekend in Atlanta or Austin. This weekend they were doing a quick date night in Miami. It was Saturday morning and Alexis was sitting in the airport waiting on her flight. She posted her customary travel photo to show off her outfit. It was cold in Atlanta so she would be a bit overdressed for Miami weather. However, she would make the necessary adjustments once they arrived. They weren't staying overnight but Enrique reserved a hotel room for them to change clothes. They would do a little sightseeing, have a picnic in the park, and later that day they would have dinner on the water. Alexis was excited. She had bought a new dress just for the occasion.

Enrique paced the floor back and forth at the airport. Why was he nervous? It made no sense to him. Alexis was the most important person in the world to him. He had proven that to himself and her time and time again. He had already gotten her dad and mom's blessing. Hell, he had gone as far as to get her siblings' blessings as well. He knew there wasn't another soul in this world designed for him. With all that assurance, he was still nervous. He kept going back to the fact that she had been proposed to before. What if she said no? What if this triggered something in her? What if? This wasn't usually who he was, but he needed this moment to go right. He boarded his flight and wished it wasn't so early because he could use some bourbon or scotch right now. He did what he had become accustomed to doing and that was writing how he felt in the journal.

Alexis and Enrique landed within twenty minutes of each other. Her flight arrived first so she made her way down to the gate Enrique was scheduled to fly into. She sat patiently waiting for him to exit. He was one of the first ones to exit and she jumped up to greet him. He was taken aback at her making a mad dash for him. He chuckled and kissed her forehead.

"Hey, babe. I see someone is excited to see me."

"I'm always excited to see you, Enrique."

Enrique moved them to the right so other passengers could continue to make their way around them.

"How was your flight?" Alexis asked.

"It was smooth. Took me too long to get to you but I'm here now," Enrique responded.

"Yes, what's the first thing we are doing?" Alexis quizzed.

"We'll pick up a rental car, go get some breakfast and head to the hotel. I have an early check-in," Enrique replied.

"Great," Alexis said.

Alexis noticed he seemed less relaxed but she didn't put too much thought into it. It was pretty early for both of them. While Enrique was a morning person, she was not. He must not have had his coffee yet.

They headed to the rental car counter and picked up the vehicle Enrique reserved and headed to a popular breakfast spot in downtown Miami. Alexis hoped it wasn't a long wait because she was starving but that was nothing new. It was evident by the ten or so pounds she had gained over the course of the last three months. Life was a lot less stressful with Enrique in it and she was happy. Really happy.

After grabbing breakfast, they headed to the hotel but decided to make a detour to the grocery store so they could pick up the items needed for the picnic later that day. As much as Alexis' appetite had increased over the last few months, eating three big meals a day was a struggle for her. She would go light with lunch so she could enjoy dinner. Apparently, the restaurant they were going to for dinner was very popular and came highly recommended so she wanted to make sure she had an appetite. They rested for a while in the room and enjoyed each other's company. Alexis noticed that Enrique seemed a little off. He was attentive but she could tell something was bothering him.

"Hey, is everything okay? You seem to be in deep thought."

"Yeah, everything is good. I'm just thinking about how far we have come since meeting in Spaln."

"You didn't think you would still be dealing with me, huh?"

"Oh no, my brown skin girl. I knew I would still be dealing with you. Didn't realize it would come with extra stuff but I wouldn't have it any other way."

"Yeah, it was crazy for a while. I appreciate everything you did to ensure I was safe."

"Always. You are mine. Don't forget it."

"I'm sure you won't let me."

Soon, it was time to head to the park for the picnic. Miami was a bit cooler than Alexis expected.

"Do you really want to go to the park in this cool air?" Enrique asked.

"Not really," Alexis responded honestly.

"Well, what do you want to do if we skip the park?" Enrique asked.

"You. I really want to do you," Alexis responded with a grin.

"And I'm all yours."

Alexis and Enrique spent the afternoon in the hotel making love and enjoying each other's company. Once they finally pried themselves out of the bed, they began getting dressed for dinner. Reservations were for seven o'clock so they needed to get a move on. Alexis dressed in her emerald, green sequin dress. The dress was long sleeved with a plunging neckline with the back out. She accessorized with gold earrings, a bracelet, and a teardrop necklace. She also wore gold pumps and a gold clutch. She did a natural look with her makeup and wore a twist out on her hair. She wouldn't be Alexis if she didn't have her signature red lipstick.

She glanced over in the mirror and was pleased with her look. She was also pleased that those extra ten pounds or so had gone to all the right places. She was looking thick, thick as Brooklyn would say. She looked over at Enrique and her breath caught in her throat. He was handsome in his black tuxedo with his massive curls pulled back into a neat ponytail. He was so damn fine and she was grateful that she still got butterflies with him. She smiled at him and he returned her smile. He was the most handsome man she had ever laid eyes on.

They made it to the restaurant with seven minutes to spare. Had it been up to Alexis they would have skipped the dinner reservations. It had taken a lot of self-control for them to keep their hands off each other but Enrique was insistent on making the reservation. Alexis would have been fine with ordering take out and feasting on each other the rest of the night. But once they arrived she was glad they kept the reservations. The view was amazing.

They opted to sit on the patio. The stars twinkled in the sky and the water was calm. While it was cooler than Alexis preferred, she didn't want to miss the view. There were only a few couples braving the cool air outdoors. She and Enrique sat and talked while they waited on their entrees. She ordered a tuna dish and Enrique ordered scallops and other seafood. The food finally arrived and they were silent until it was all eaten.

"This food was delicious. How were the scallops? Not that I should ask since you didn't leave a trace behind."

"They were amazing. Some of the best I've had in a while. You want dessert?"

"Of course, what kind of question is that? I won't turn down dessert."

"Okay, order dessert and I'm going to head to the restroom."

"Do you want something?"

"No, I'll have some of whatever you get."

"Okay."

Alexis ordered dessert. She also noticed that Enrique was taking a while to come back. She hoped he was feeling okay. He had scarfed down a lot of food in a short amount of time. Just as the waitress came out with the dessert Enrique came out walking behind her.

"Thank you," Alexis replied to the waitress. She then looked at Enrique, "I thought I was going to have to come find you. Are you okay?"

"Yes, I had to take care of something." Enrique moved his chair to the side of the table with Alexis. They looked out across the water and admired the view. "Look at that building," he pointed. "How long do you think it would take you to count all the lights in that building?"

"Forever," Alexis responded.

"Speaking of forever," Enrique said as he got down on one knee. "That's exactly how long I want to spend my life with you. Alexis Carter, will you marry me?"

Alexis was so overwhelmed with emotion. She could barely say anything but she managed a, "Yes!"

So much was happening so fast that Alexis didn't have time to register everything that was taking place. She hadn't realized the two guys that sat at the table next to them were really the videographer and photographer. The couple that sat at the other table were people Enrique hired to go live in the private Facebook group he created for their family and friends to be able to share in their special moment.

There was applause from the other two couples on the patio with them. Alexis and Enrique stood side by side and took pictures. Once they were done, they said hi to family and friends in the Facebook group. She was blown away because she had no idea, but she appreciated every moment of it. It was intimate and so thoughtful. There was no doubt in her mind that she was ready to be Mrs. Enrique Manuel. This time everything felt different. It felt right.

Enrique had gotten it right with the ring, too. It was a three carat, solitaire, 14K white gold diamond ring. Alexis playfully rolled her eyes. It was just like him to go over the top because he wanted the world to know she was his. There would be no denying that she was taken because the ring could be spotted a mile away. She made up her mind at that moment that she didn't want a long engagement but she would save that conversation for another time. Right now, she wanted to enjoy the moment and her man. Her soon to be husband that she'd met by chance in a Spanish restaurant.

PROLOGUe

Two years later…

Alexis and Enrique stood in the courtyard of the boutique hotel in Madrid. Enrique stood behind Alexis as he rubbed her very pregnant belly. It was hard to believe they would be parents to a precious baby boy soon. Not just any baby boy but to his namesake. They decided they would call him EJ. Enrique was going to be a dad and he could hardly wait. Alexis was the most gorgeous pregnant woman he had ever laid eyes on but then she was the most gorgeous woman he had ever laid eyes on.

At that moment they were being photographed and not for a maternity shoot. Alexis agreed to spend the latter half of her pregnancy in Spain so the baby could have dual citizenship like Enrique. Her mom was scheduled to fly out in a couple weeks as her due date was getting closer. She would spend the first six months in Madrid before heading back to Austin. Enrique said he would fly back and forth but Alexis knew there was no way he would leave her and EJ for any amount of time. She knew for sure he wouldn't leave them in another country. She thought he was overprotective before but now it was borderline insane. It could be a bit overwhelming from time to time but she loved his passion to protect her and now them at all costs.

So much happened in two years. Shortly after Alexis and Enrique's wedding, his mom announced she would be moving soon. Unbeknownst to either of them, Rose made the decision to move back to Madrid. The move didn't happen right away but about eight months after the wedding, Rose began the process. She hung around a little longer once she realized that Alexis was pregnant and she decided when they went the latter months of the pregnancy that she would leave permanently. At first, it seemed a little haste but once Enrique realized his mom and dad were working to rekindle their relationship it made sense. They weren't just rekindling because technically they had never given up on the relationship.

So, here they are. Alexis and Enrique, standing in the courtyard where his parents will take their vows in front of family and friends in a couple of hours. At his mother's request, they were doing a photoshoot for her. Life was good. Alexis was happy and was living well with her husband, new family, and soon to be baby boy.

Alexis realized she didn't have to do anything to get even with all the drama from her past. The perfect revenge is living well…